Anastasia Off Her Rocker

Lois Lowry

Houghton Mifflin Harcourt
Boston New York

 Originally published in hardcover in the United States as *Anastasia, Ask Your Analyst,* by Houghton Mifflin Books for Children, an imprint of Houghton Mifflin Harcourt Publishing Company, 1984.

www.hmhco.com

The Library of Congress has cataloged the hardcover edition as follows:
Lowry, Lois.
Anastasia, ask your analyst.
Summary: Anastasia's seventh-grade science project becomes almost more than she can handle, but brother Sam, age three, and a bust of Freud, aid her nobly.
[1. Gerbils—Fiction. 2. Brothers and sisters—Fiction.]
I. Title.
PZ7.L9673Amc 1984 [Fic] 83-26687

ISBN: 978-0-395-36011-0 hardcover
ISBN: 978-0-544-43959-7 paperback

Manufactured in the U.S.A.
DOC 10 9 8 7 6 5 4 3 2 1

4500534575

For the child in Nebraska
who wrote and suggested
that the Krupniks should have pets,
and Sam should have
a friend

one

"Mom!" shouted Anastasia as she clattered up the back steps and into the kitchen after school. "Guess what Meredith Halberg gave me! Just what I've been wanting! And it didn't cost *anything!*"

Mrs. Krupnik put a casserole into the oven, closed the oven door, and adjusted the temperature. She turned around. "Let me think," she said. "Chicken-pox?"

Anastasia made a face. It was terrible, having a mother who always made jokes. "Ha ha, very funny," she said. "I said it was something I'd been *wanting.* Anyway, I had chickenpox years ago."

"Well," said her mother, "I can't think of anything else that doesn't cost anything."

Anastasia was so excited she was almost jumping up and down. "You'll never guess! Wait, I'll show you. They're on the back porch. They're probably getting cold. I'll bring them in."

"Hold it," her mother said. She looked suspicious. "What do you mean, they're getting cold? It's not something *alive,* is it?"

But Anastasia had already gone, banging the door behind her. In a minute she was back, holding a wooden box with a wire mesh cover over it. A rustling sound came from inside the box.

Her mother retreated instantly, behind the kitchen table. "No!" she said. "It *is* something alive! Anastasia, absolutely not! I've told you and told you that I can't stand—"

Anastasia wasn't listening. Her mother was so boring sometimes. She undid the latch and lifted the cover of the box.

"*Gerbils!*" she announced with delight.

Her mother backed away until she was against the refrigerator. She picked up a wooden spoon and held it like a weapon. "GET THOSE THINGS OUT OF MY KITCHEN IMMEDIATELY!" she bellowed.

"But, Mom, look how cute they are—"

"I SAID, OUT OF MY KITCHEN!"

Grouchily, Anastasia covered the box again. She took it to the back hall.

"Mom," she said when she returned, "you can open your eyes now. They're in the back hall."

Her mother sat down and took some deep breaths. She looked around warily. "Anastasia," she said, "you know I can't stand rodents."

"Mom, they're sweet, furry little—"

"Rodents." Her mother shuddered.

"Well, maybe. But, Mom—"

Her mother laid the wooden spoon on the table. She took another deep breath. "Rodents make me faint," she said. "I very nearly passed right out cold when you started taking the lid off that box."

Anastasia sighed. There wasn't another kid in the whole town who had a mother so idiotic. Coffee, she thought. Coffee will help. She took the coffeepot from the stove and poured her mother a cup.

"Let's have a reasonable conversation about this subject," she suggested, handing her mother the cup of steaming coffee.

Her mother sipped, and shuddered one more time. "Tell me one reasonable reason for having disgusting rodents in this house," she said grimly.

"I can tell you lots more than one. The first is that I really need a pet."

"You have one. You've had Frank Goldfish since you were eight years old. I thought you loved Frank."

"I *do* love Frank, but he's boring. You can't teach him tricks. You can't cuddle him."

"You want to teach tricks to—you want to *cuddle* those—what are they called?"

"Romeo and Juliet. I named them on the way home."

"I don't mean *names.* I meant—what did you say they are?"

"Gerbils."

"Okay, then. If you want to teach tricks to gerbils, I suggest you start by teaching them to walk on their cute, furry little hind legs. Right through the back door, down the steps, across the street, around the corner, and back to Meredith Halberg's house."

"Mom, that's *stupid.*"

Her mother sighed. "I know it's stupid. But, Anastasia, honestly, I have this rodent phobia."

"I can see that. You look very pale. I'm really concerned about you, Mom. That's why it's important to get used to Romeo and Juliet and overcome this very serious phobia that you have."

Her mother groaned. At least she wasn't screaming "no" anymore. That was a good sign.

"Reason number two," said Anastasia. "They're going to be my science project. The Science Fair is in February, and I'm the only kid in the seventh grade who hasn't chosen a project yet."

"I told you to do the life cycle of the frog. I *told* you I'd help you make a huge poster describing the life cycle of the frog."

"For Pete's sake, Mom, that's something you do in third grade. Everybody in the entire world has already done the life cycle of the frog, in third grade. This is junior high. This guy in my class—Norman Berkowitz? He's building a *computer* for his science project."

"Norman Berkowitz's father won the Nobel Prize in Physics last year," Mrs. Krupnik pointed out. She got up and poured herself another cup of coffee.

"Well," said Anastasia sulkily, "so what. Big deal. Dad was nominated for the American Book Award last year. The daughter of the person who was nominated for the American Book Award can't turn up at the Science Fair with a dumb life cycle of the frog poster, for Pete's sake."

"What on earth could you do with a couple of smelly rodents?"

"They're not smelly," said Anastasia angrily. "I'm going to mate my gerbils, and then—"

"You're going to *what?*"

"*Mate* my gerbils. Then I'll study the pregnancy, and make notes, and observe their babies. I'll learn everything to know about—"

"OVER MY DEAD BODY ARE YOU GOING TO MATE RODENTS IN THIS HOUSE."

Whoops. She was losing ground, Anastasia knew. Time to present reason number three.

"Mom," she said calmly, "you're being unreasonable and irrational again. Here's reason number three. Think about Sam."

"I *am* thinking about Sam," said Mrs. Krupnik forcefully. "I do not want a three-year-old playing with nasty, filthy, little—"

"Mom, gerbils are *clean.* Be calm now. You know

how you're always saying that sex education should begin in the home."

Her mother was starting to take deep breaths again, a bad sign. She sipped her coffee. "That's true," she said. "I do say that. What does that have to do with rodents?"

"Gerbils. Practice saying *gerbils,* Mom."

"Gerbils, then. What about sex education and gerbils? And what about Sam?"

"It's Sam's chance for sex education—right here in his very own home! He can see my gerbils having babies! Sam doesn't know anything about sex yet."

"Anastasia," her mother said and sighed. "Sam's not *interested* in sex. He's only three."

"But he's super intelligent, Mom. You know how interested he is in everything. You know how he's starting to learn to read, and he knows all the letters, and all the numbers, and—"

"That has nothing to do with sex."

"I bet you *anything* that Sam is very interested in sex."

"Bet you he isn't."

Anastasia thought for a minute. If she did this right, she would win. But it would be tricky.

"Where is Sam?" she asked casually.

"In the living room, playing."

"Tell you what," Anastasia suggested. "Let's ask him. Let's ask him if he's interested in sex, and if he says yes, can I keep Romeo and Juliet?"

"No way," said her mother. "It wouldn't be fair, because the instant he sees them, he'll *say* he's interested."

"I won't let him see them. I won't even mention gerbils. It'll be a fair test."

Her mother gulped the last of her coffee while she thought it over. Finally she said, "Okay, but here are the rules. I'll call Sam in, and I'll ask him. And you are not to say a word about gerbils or gerbil babies. Not one word, understand?"

Anastasia nodded. "I won't. We'll only ask him if he's interested in sex."

"I'll ask him. You keep your mouth completely shut."

Anastasia clamped her mouth closed. She sucked her lips in between her teeth.

Her mother examined the clamped-mouth face. "Okay," she said.

She put her empty coffee cup in the sink, went to the kitchen door, and called, "Sam? Would you come in here for a minute? I want to ask you something."

They could hear Sam's little feet trotting down the hall. He appeared in the kitchen door, grinning, with his blue jeans sagging and his sneakers untied.

"Hi, Anastasia!" Sam said. "Today at nursery school I did blocks. All the blocks have letters. I can spell my name with blocks, and I can spell 'airplane,' and 'cookie,' and—"

Anastasia smiled at him and didn't say anything. She kept her mouth clamped closed.

"Sam, old buddy," said Mrs. Krupnik casually, "I have a question I want to ask you."

"Okay," said Sam happily. "Can I have a cookie?"

Anastasia handed him a raisin cookie from the cookie jar. She kept her mouth tightly closed.

"Sam," said his mother, "are you interested in sex?"

Sam had stuffed half a cookie into his mouth. He chewed solemnly.

"Sam?" asked his mother.

"I'm thinking," he said, with his mouth full. "I'm giving it serious thought."

Finally, after he had swallowed, he asked, "How do you spell it?"

Anastasia grinned. Victory was in sight. She began to open her mouth to say "S." But her mother glared at her.

"Anastasia," Mrs. Krupnik said in warning, "keep your mouth absolutely shut, or our bet is off."

To Sam, Mrs. Krupnik said, "S-E-X."

Sam chewed the other half of his cookie slowly. He frowned. He was thinking. You could always tell when Sam was thinking because his forehead wrinkled up.

"I'll be back in a minute," he said suddenly, and trotted out of the kitchen.

Anastasia sat very still with her mouth tightly closed. Her lips were beginning to ache.

Then Sam reappeared. "Yes," he announced. "I am *very* interested in sex." And off he went, back to his game in the living room.

Mrs. Krupnik stared at Anastasia. Her eyes narrowed into a suspicious look. "All right," she said, finally. "A bet's a bet. You win."

Anastasia relaxed her mouth and wiggled her tongue a bit to make sure it still worked. She grinned. "Thanks, Mom," she said.

"You tricked me somehow. Tell me how."

Anastasia took a cookie and began to pick the raisins out, one by one. She popped them into her mouth. She didn't say anything.

"Why am I always outsmarted by a thirteen-year-old? Tell me how you did it!"

Finally Anastasia shrugged. "It wasn't a trick. It was just that I've been teaching Sam to play Scrabble. I knew when he left the kitchen that he was going off to check the Scrabble points in 'sex.' *X* is one of his favorite letters. Eight points for an *X*." She broke off a bit of the raisinless cookie and put it in her mouth.

Her mother watched her chew. After a moment she said, "Someday, Anastasia, I am going to offer you for adoption."

"Me and my gerbils, right?"

Science Project

Anastasia Krupnik
Mr. Sherman's Class

On October 13, I acquired two wonderful little gerbils, who are living in a cage in my bedroom. Their names are Romeo and Juliet, and they are very friendly. They seem to like each other a lot. Since they are living in the same cage as man and wife, I expect they will have gerbil babies. My gerbil book says that it takes twenty-five days to make gerbil babies. I think they are already mating, because they act very affectionate to each other, so I will count today as DAY ONE and then I will observe them for twenty-five days and I hope that on DAY 25 their babies will be born.

This will be my Science Project.

"What are you writing?" asked Sam. He was on his knees on Anastasia's bedroom floor, one arm in the gerbil cage as he stroked the heads of the furry creatures with his fingers.

"My science project for school," Anastasia explained. "I'm telling about Romeo and Juliet."

Sam looked up and frowned. "These are partly my gerbils, right?" he asked.

"Sure. It was because of you that I got to keep them. So I guess they're partly yours."

"Well, I want to name one Prince," said Sam.

Anastasia made a face. "Prince is a dog's name," she said.

Sam sighed. "Yeah," he said. "I really wanted a dog. I could *play* with a dog."

"You can play with the gerbils. Gerbils are friendly."

"These gerbils aren't. Look. They're biting each other." Sam pointed his finger into the cage.

Anastasia looked. Sam was right. The two gerbils were tussling with each other, their little teeth exposed.

"That's a domestic fight, I think," she told her brother. "Like when Mom and Dad have an argument. These gerbils are husband and wife, so of course they have little fights now and then."

Sam looked at the gerbils dubiously. "They're kind of ugly," he said. "And they're fat."

Anastasia closed her notebook and sighed. "Quit complaining, Sam. They're fat because they eat a lot. And they're not ugly."

"That one," said Sam, pointing, "is very, very ugly. Can I name that one Nicky?"

"No," said Anastasia impatiently. "Why on earth would you name a gerbil Nicky?"

"Because it looks like an ugly kid at my nursery school. Nicky. Nicky is the ugliest person I know. And fat, too. Nicky is very fat and very ugly, just like these gerbils, and Nicky also bites."

Anastasia glanced out of her bedroom window, down into the yard where her father was raking leaves. "Sam," she said, "why don't you go down to the yard? Maybe Dad will let you jump into the leaf piles."

"Are you going to come and jump in leaf piles with me?"

"No," Anastasia sighed. "I have to stay here and observe the gerbils. For my science project. Close the door when you leave. I promised Mom that she would never hear one single gerbil noise from my room."

Sam latched the lid of the cage and headed for the door. "I wish you were doing a dog for your science project," he said wistfully, "so I could name it Prince."

two

Anastasia came in from school, dropped her books on the kitchen table, rummaged through the refrigerator until she found something that looked appealing—a piece of cold chicken, which she dipped in some mustard—and then headed up the back stairs to her room.

At the closed door of her bedroom she stopped, startled. Her way was blocked by the vacuum cleaner, which was sitting in the middle of the hall floor. Attached to it with a piece of Scotch tape was a note.

"Anastasia," the note said. "You realize that I can't possibly clean your room anymore, since you have those things in there, and I suffer from this phobia. Be sure to do in the corners, and under the bed. Put the vacuum cleaner away in the hall closet when you're done. Love, Mom."

"Love, Mom"? Did Hitler sign notes "Love, Adolf"?

Anastasia glowered, and went back downstairs in search of her mother. "Love, Mom," indeed!

Mrs. Krupnik, wearing jeans and a paint-spattered man's shirt, was sitting on the floor of the room that she used as her artist's studio. Beside her was Sam, squatting on his short three-year-old legs. His face and clothes and hands were daubed with different colors. He grinned up at Anastasia and then went back to stirring a coffee can filled with bright orange paint.

There were oatmeal boxes all over the floor of the big room, on top of newspapers. Two of the boxes had been painted bright blue; the others were waiting. The Quaker Oats man was smiling his patronizing smile at Anastasia. That was all she needed, to be leered at by Mr. Quaker Oats when she was *already* furious.

"I hate that guy's looks," Anastasia said, frowning. "He looks so *wholesome.* I wish someone would make him eat sugary cereal filled with chemical additives."

"Goodness. Why are you so grouchy?" asked Katherine Krupnik.

"Three guesses," said Anastasia, glaring at her mother.

Mrs. Krupnik picked up one of the empty boxes, studied the Quaker Oats man for a minute, and then painted an orange mustache on his face with a flourish. "I think he's cute," she said. "He has a benevolent look. I like Quakers in general. I just wish I liked oatmeal better. It's taken two years to save up these boxes."

"I SAID, THREE GUESSES," Anastasia repeated loudly.

Her mother smiled at her pleasantly. "I don't want to discuss it," she said. "You told me you'd keep them completely out of my sight. Okay. That means you clean your own room, kiddo."

"We're making a train!" announced Sam gleefully. "The blue ones are going to be the boxcars, and now we're going to do orange, and they'll be the— What are they going to be, Mom?"

"Cattle cars," said Mrs. Krupnik. "And we'll have a green coal car, and a black engine with silver trimming, and of course the caboose will be red—"

She interrupted herself. "Here, Sam," she said, handing him the box she was holding, "take this one with the mustache and paint the whole box orange."

Anastasia scowled. "What's for dinner?" she asked.

Her mother was blowing on the blue boxes to dry them. She looked up. "Dinner? What time is it?"

"Almost five. I stayed late at school because stupid Daphne has a crush on a guy on the stupid football team, and she made me stay and watch stupid football practice with her."

Mrs. Krupnik sighed and wiped her hands on a rag. "I forgot all about dinner, Anastasia. I forgot to take anything out of the freezer. I was so excited about making this train because I'd been saving the boxes for almost two years. This morning when Sam was at nursery school, I opened a closet door and all these oatmeal boxes fell out at me, and I realized I had enough, finally, and so when Sam got home, we— Sam, did we ever have lunch?"

Sam was painting the Quaker Oats man industriously. His tongue was wedged between his teeth. There was an orange spot on his nose. "Yeah," he told her. "Hot dogs."

Anastasia's mother put the rag down and stood

up. "Dinner," she said. "Dinner. Let's see. You know what? In order to get that one last box, the one for the caboose, I emptied out a batch of Quaker Oats into a plastic bag. Maybe I could—"

"MOM!" wailed Anastasia. "I don't want oatmeal for dinner! I *hate* oatmeal!"

"I don't," said Sam cheerfully. "I *love* oatmeal, because it makes me get a train."

Anastasia headed angrily toward the door of the studio. "I'm going to the kitchen," she announced, "and I'm going to examine the contents of the refrigerator, and there had better be something in there that we can have for dinner. Because it's against the law to starve your family, Mom. If I call this special phone number that I know about—this phone number you call if you know of a Very Troubled Family—they'll send social workers to investigate."

Her mother laughed. "We have eggs," she said. "I'll make an omelet. I'll put cheese in it, and onions, and green peppers, and I think I have some mushrooms. Your social worker would arrive, Anastasia, and it would smell so good that she'd want to be invited for dinner."

"Ketchup," said Sam. "Put ketchup on it, too."

Anastasia sniffed. It was a sort of sniff that she'd been practicing in her room, a huffy sort of noise she could do with her nose, which meant "I am above this sort of thing." It was the kind of sniff that she imagined Queen Elizabeth would do if Diana asked her to change William's diapers.

"Mother," she said, "I would like to have a private conversation with you. I would like to have it now, before Dad gets home, and I don't want Sam there, either, because it is a *female* conversation."

Her mother sighed, dropped her paintbrush into a can of water, and said, "Sam, you keep doing the orange, okay? You can probably get two more boxes done before it's time to get cleaned up for dinner."

Sam nodded solemnly, his tongue between his teeth again.

Mrs. Krupnik followed Anastasia down the hall to the kitchen. Anastasia's feet went thump, thump, thump; partly because she was upset, and partly because she was wearing her very favorite heavy hiking boots. Her mother's feet made no sound at all because her mother was barefoot. There was bright blue paint on Katherine Krupnik's toes.

They sat down on two kitchen chairs, facing each other across the round table.

"What's up?" asked Mrs. Krupnik cheerfully. "Got female troubles?"

"No," said Anastasia in a grim voice. "*You* do."

"*Me?* A healthy, happy, lovable person like me?"

Even though she was still angry, Anastasia began to feel a twinge of sympathy. Her mother didn't even *realize* she had this problem. I'll be gentle with her, she decided.

"Mom," she said as gently as she could, "I believe you are entering menopause."

"Beer," her mother said, after a long silence. She stood up and opened the refrigerator. "I am going to have a beer."

"Typical," murmured Anastasia. "Typical escape mechanism."

Her mother opened the can with a hiss, took a drink, and made a face. "Yuck," she said. "I hate beer. But I hate this conversation even more. What on earth do you mean, Anastasia?"

Anastasia picked up the salt shaker, sprinkled some salt in the palm of her hand, poked it with a finger, and licked her finger. It was a thing she always did when she was thinking; at least if she was thinking in the kitchen. You needed something to do with your hands if you were thinking heavy, painful thoughts.

"Mom," she said finally, "you're becoming very weird."

Her mother took another sip of beer and made another face. "Tell me what you mean by that," she said at last.

"It's kind of hard to describe," Anastasia began.

"I can imagine. Please try, though."

"Well, I used to like you a whole lot. I thought you were a really neat mother. You used to be fun. But lately—"

"Yes? Go on. Tell me about lately." Her mother sipped again. This time she didn't even make a face.

"Well, your clothes, for example. They're embarrassing. You always wear jeans. I don't even like to walk beside you on the street because you don't look like a regular mother."

"I see," said her mother tersely. "And what else?"

"You're always doing stupid stuff. Like the fuss about my poor little gerbils, for example. The note on the vacuum cleaner. What if I'd had a friend with me? What if a friend of mine had seen that note on the vacuum cleaner? And for Pete's sake, Mom, then I find you on the floor with a billion oatmeal boxes, making a dumb train. What if a friend has seen *that?* I can't even think about how embarrassed I would have been if I'd brought a friend home with me today. I don't want my friends to know the kind of stupid stuff you do." Anastasia licked a little more salt from her fingertip. She was beginning to feel perfectly miserable.

"And all of this has just started lately, you say?" asked her mother.

"Yeah. It's only been, oh, say the last couple of weeks."

"But I told you that I'd been saving those oatmeal boxes for almost two years. Since Sam was just an infant. Wouldn't you call that weird and stupid—saving oatmeal boxes to make a train? But you said I was fine until recently."

"Well, I just began to notice it recently," muttered Anastasia, looking at the floor.

"And I've always worn jeans. I'm a painter, so it makes sense for me to wear jeans. You want me to wear a tweed suit while I stand at an easel?"

Anastasia didn't know how to answer. Finally she said, almost in a whisper, "I wish you wouldn't be a painter. I wish you'd just be a normal mother."

"Like who? Give me an example."

"Well, Daphne's mother. She always wears a dress, and makeup—"

"Makeup makes my face itch."

"—and when we go to Daphne's house after school, her mother is always having tea with someone, or playing bridge. And she teaches Sunday school."

"Anastasia, that's normal for Daphne's mother. She's the wife of the Congregational minister. But it wouldn't be normal for *me.* Normal is different for different people, don't you see that?"

Anastasia kicked the table leg with her hiking boot. She sighed. "I don't like your kind of normal," she said miserably.

Her mother leaned back in her chair. She scratched the sole of one bare foot by rubbing it across her jeans. She sipped her beer. She thought. She began to smile a little.

"Anastasia," she said, "I believe I know what's wrong. I want you to think for a minute about your friends. And give me honest answers, promise?"

"I'm always honest."

"True. Okay. Think for a minute about Daphne Bellingham. Does she think her mother is terrific?"

"No," Anastasia admitted. "She thinks her mother is weird and disgusting."

"Meredith Halberg. What does she think of her mother?"

Anastasia groaned. "She can't stand her mother. Because her mother has a Danish accent, and it's so embarrassing. She told her mother never to talk if she brings her friends home from school." Anastasia giggled.

"One more. Sonya. What's her last name, that cute little friend of yours named Sonya?"

"Isaacson. Well, *her* mother—good grief. Well, her mother dyes her hair *orange.*"

"Gross and embarrassing, right?"

"Of course."

Anastasia's mother started to chuckle. She put down her beer can, still almost full, as if she didn't need it anymore. "Sweetie," she said. "Let me explain to you what's wrong. I should have realized it much sooner than this. You say this all started just a couple of weeks ago?"

"More or less. At least that's when I began to notice it."

"Remember what happened a couple of weeks ago?"

Anastasia shrugged. "Nothing much. I did lousy on a math test. I went to a garage sale with Sonya and Meredith, and Dad yelled at me because I spent five dollars on junk. There's another garage sale this Saturday, Mom, so I'm warning you that I may spend money on junk again."

"Don't you remember that Dad and I took you to dinner at a Chinese restaurant?"

"Yeah. So what? There was something in the sweet-and-sour pork that made you turn weird?"

"Nope." Her mother grinned. "Why did we take you out to dinner?"

"What is this, Twenty Questions? It was my birthday. My thirteenth birthday."

"Right. And how old are your friends? How old is Daphne?"

"Thirteen."

"Sonya?"

"Thirteen."

"Meredith?"

"Almost thirteen. What does that have to do with anything?"

Her mother got up and began to take eggs out of the refrigerator. She was still grinning. "I'd forgotten. How can I be a mother and forget something so important?"

"*What,* Mom? I hate it when you act mysterious."

"It's something that happens around the time you become thirteen. It happened to *me.* I had a much worse case than you do; how can I have forgotten that? My mother and grandmother took me to New York City for the day when I was thirteen, and I wanted to die, I was so embarrassed. My mother had this coat with a fur collar, and it looked as if she had some kind of animal wrapped around her neck; it was so disgusting. And my grandmother wore a wig, and had a Russian accent. I walked as far away from them as I could, so that I could pretend they were strangers."

"I don't know what you're talking about. People's mothers change and become disgusting when people are thirteen?"

"Nope. The mothers stay the same, but the thirteen-year-olds change, and the mothers *seem* disgusting."

"It happens to everybody?"

"I'm sure of it. I bet anything that in Alaska, thirteen-year-old Eskimo girls get together and talk about how weird their mothers are. In China. Africa. Everywhere."

"Why? Why does it happen?"

Anastasia's mother was whisking the eggs together in a bowl. "Gosh, I don't really know. I bet it's hormones. When people begin to mature physically, all those hormones start rushing around, or something."

"Well," said Anastasia angrily, "they ought to *warn* you. All those dumb books they give you to read, about getting your period and stuff. That's just *normal* stuff. Why don't they warn you about the *abnormal* stuff, like you'll start to hate your mother?"

"You know what? I think they do. Wasn't there a chapter in that book you had? A chapter called 'Emotional Changes' or something like that?"

Anastasia groaned. "Yeah," she acknowledged. "But I didn't read it, because it looked boring. The whole *book* was boring, but that chapter looked like the most boring of all, except maybe for the one called 'Personal Hygiene.' So I didn't even read it. And now it turns out that the most important stuff was in there."

"Well," said her mother, "reading it probably wouldn't have helped much, because you would still feel that way anyway. You'd still hate me," she said cheerfully, and began chopping a green pepper.

Anastasia stared at the floor. She was consumed with gloom. Completely consumed. "What can I do about it?" she asked. "Is there a cure?"

"Time. Wait it out. In the meantime, sweets, would you go get Sam cleaned up for dinner?"

Anastasia slammed the salt shaker down on the table. She stood up. "Why is it," she asked loudly, "that I always have to chase after that brat and change his yucky wet pants and wash his grubby hands? Nobody else's mother makes their kid do that kind of stuff. Nobody but *you.* Of all the mothers in the world, I had to get stuck with the only one who—"

She stopped short. Her mother was shaking with laughter.

"AND DON'T LAUGH!" roared Anastasia. She

stomped out of the kitchen and up the stairs. At the door to her bedroom she stopped and gave the vacuum cleaner a swift kick that sent it thumping onto its side. She went into her room and slammed the door.

Science Project

Anastasia Krupnik
Mr. Sherman's Class

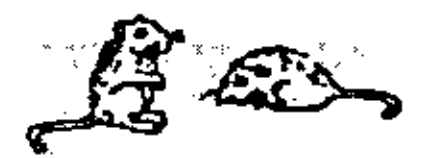

On October 13, I acquired two wonderful little gerbils, who are living in a cage in my bedroom. Their names are Romeo and Juliet, and they are very friendly. They seem to like each other a lot. Since they are living in the same cage as man and wife, I expect they will have gerbil babies. My gerbil book says that it takes twenty-five days to make gerbil babies. I think they are already mating, because they act very affectionate to each other, so I will count today as DAY ONE and then I will observe them for twenty-five days and I hope that on DAY 25 their babies will be born.

This will be my Science Project.

Day Three.

My gerbils haven't changed much. They lie in their cage and sleep a lot. They're both overweight, because they eat too much, and they resemble Sonya Isaacson's mother, at least in chubbiness.

In personality, they resemble *my* mother. They're very grouchy.

Anastasia put her pencil down, and sighed. She glanced at the gerbils. They weren't as much fun as she had thought they would be. Maybe when Juliet had her babies in—Anastasia counted—twenty-two more days, if things worked the way they were supposed to . . .

Sam knocked at her door. He poked his head inside.

"You're supposed to get me cleaned up for dinner," he said. There was orange paint in his hair, on his clothes, and all over his face.

Grudgingly Anastasia took his hand and headed with him toward the bathroom.

"Why is the vacuum cleaner all tipped over in the hall?" Sam asked innocently.

"I do not care to discuss it," said Anastasia in her Queen Elizabeth voice.

three

It was amazing, Anastasia thought as she ate, how her mother could turn a lot of *nothing* into a decent dinner. After school, when she had found the piece of cold chicken to gnaw on, the refrigerator had looked almost totally empty to her. It looked like the kind of refrigerator that might belong to starving peasants in India: a couple cans of beer, a carton of eggs, and a few plastic containers of leftovers. In the shelves on the inside of the door were all those things that lived in refrigerators for centuries: mustard, ketchup, mayonnaise, horseradish, and salad dressing.

And in the drawer at the bottom, the drawer that said CRISPER on it, was nothing but a folder full of poems. Her father was almost finished writing a new book of poetry, and he always kept his unfinished manuscripts in the refrigerator drawer, the place where normal people kept lettuce. He said that if the house ever burned down, the refrigerator probably wouldn't burn, so his unpublished book would be safe.

There had been a time—when she was younger and more naive—Anastasia had thought that was really neat. During that time she had always opened the refrigerator when friends were visiting, to show them the crisper full of poems, with great pride.

"Oh," she would say casually, when her friends were surprised, "doesn't your dad keep his manuscripts in the refrigerator?" And they would say no, their dad didn't write poems; their dad was a computer programmer, or a lawyer, or an electrician. Closing the refrigerator again, Anastasia would respond politely: "Pity." Just the way Queen Elizabeth would.

But lately she'd been embarrassed by the refrigerator drawer. She always hoped, when friends were over, that they would never go looking for a carrot.

So it wasn't only her *mother,* Anastasia realized, who was a source of embarrassment now. It was her father, too. And Sam, of course. Sam was a huge, humongous humiliation. His pants were usually wet, his face was always dirty, and—most humiliating of all—he had an IQ of about a billion. He was teaching himself to read, for Pete's sake, and he was only three years old. And he could *type.* Talk about embarrassing!

Once, shortly after school had begun, and Anastasia was beginning to make friends here in the new town that they had just moved to in the summer, Sonya Isaacson had come home with her in the afternoon. The door to the study had been closed, and through it they could hear the sound of typing.

"Your father must be in there writing a book," Sonya Isaacson had said in awe, because Anastasia had bragged a bit about what a famous writer her father was.

"I guess so," Anastasia had said. But she knew it wasn't true. Her father was teaching a seminar at Harvard that afternoon.

She had tried to hustle Sonya past the study and up the stairs to her room. But the sound of the typing stopped, and Sonya hesitated. She wanted to be a famous writer herself, so she was dying to meet Anastasia Krupnik's father, who had been nominated for the American Book Award last year.

Then the door to the study opened, and Anastasia could feel Sonya beside her, standing up straighter, ready to shake hands with the famous Myron Krupnik, who had been called Master of the Contemporary Image right on the front page of the *New York Times Book Review.*

Instead, out came Sam: barefoot, grubby, wet (though Anastasia thought maybe Sonya didn't notice the wet), and holding a piece of typing paper in his hand. He held the paper up and displayed it proudly. "I was writing a story," he announced, then he scampered off toward the kitchen.

Anastasia had made a face and nudged Sonya on up the stairs. "That's just my stupid brother," she explained. "He fools with Dad's typewriter. He likes to make asterisks."

But Sonya had gotten a good look at Sam's paper. "That wasn't asterisks," she said. "It said, 'airplane. sky. zoom. down. crash.'"

"Probably didn't have any capital letters," said Anastasia glumly. "Sam's so dumb."

But all the rest of the way up the stairs, all the way

to the third floor where Anastasia's room was, Sonya had said in a loud, astonished voice, "DUMB? You call that DUMB?"

And now, at this very moment, Sam was sitting there at the table, boosted up by two volumes of the *Encyclopedia Britannica* underneath him, and he was dumping ketchup all over a mushroom omelet. Talk about disgusting.

I need help, thought Anastasia. Mom said give it time. But *time* is not going to cure this situation.

"Dad?" she asked, looking up from her plate. "Did Mom tell you about the conversation she and I had before dinner?"

"A little," he acknowledged. "Sounds like a normal sort of problem to me. I remember having it myself when I was your age. It isn't confined to females."

Typical, Anastasia thought. *Typical,* that they don't even see the seriousness of this. "Dad," she said, "I am having a serious emotional crisis."

Sam looked up from his dinner. His face lit up with interest. "Emotional?" he asked. "I know about that!"

"Sam," said Mrs. Krupnik gently, "I don't think—"

"Yes," said Sam, nodding his head vigorously.

"Today in school we learned about emotions! Look! I'll show you the emotions I can do!"

He climbed down from his chair. Anastasia groaned. There was ketchup on Sam's bib. There was ketchup on his hands. There was even ketchup on one of Sam's ears.

Sam paused for a moment beside his own chair; then he dashed around the entire dining room table at full speed. Everyone cringed when he rounded the corner near the cabinet full of antique dishes, but he missed it by an inch.

Back at his own chair, Sam panted for a moment and then said, "That was my running emotion. Now look."

He leaped into the air and came down with a crash. The ice in Dr. Krupnik's glass of water clinked when Sam hit the floor.

"That was my jumping emotion," Sam announced. "Now watch this one."

He balanced on one sneaker and hopped halfway across the room. "Hopping emotion," he said happily.

His parents and sister were watching him in bewilderment. But suddenly Mrs. Krupnik smiled.

"Sam," she said, "you're talking about *motions.* That's not quite the same. Now come back and finish your dinner."

"Right," said Sam. He climbed back into his chair and reached for the ketchup bottle. "That was my climbing emotion," he explained. "And I can do more. When I have my bath I'll show you my swimming emotion."

Anastasia had propped both elbows on the table and put her head into her hands. I live in a family of lunatics, she thought. I may not survive.

She looked up and drew her shoulders back. "Dad," she said assertively, "and Mom, I think I ought to go to a psychiatrist."

"A *what?*" asked her father.

"A *who?*" asked her mother.

"A psychiatrist. You know: a shrink."

"Me too!" said Sam. "I want to go to a shrink too! Look at me: I'm shrinking!" Giggling, he slipped off his encyclopedia volumes and slowly disappeared under the table.

"I'm the Incredible Shrinking Man!" he called from his invisible location. "I saw it on TV."

Anastasia slammed her napkin down on the table.

"That was your shrinking emotion, right?" she said sarcastically to Sam, who was still invisible. "May I be excused? I've lost my appetite."

Her mother nodded, and Anastasia picked up her plate to take it to the kitchen.

"We'll talk about this later, sport," said her father. "After Sam's in bed."

"No," said her father firmly. "Absolutely not."

Anastasia glanced at her mother, who hadn't said anything. But her mother was shaking her head no, agreeing with her father. The traitor. Back in the old days, the good old days, her mother had very often taken her side. But now she was just sitting there agreeing with him: typical traitor behavior.

Sam was tucked away upstairs, cleaned of ketchup, reveling in the applause he'd received from his parents for his demonstration of swimming emotions in the tub. Now there was music playing softly on the stereo, and a fire was crackling in the fireplace. Anastasia's parents were sipping coffee. It was the kind of scene Anastasia used to like—when she was younger, before she became a seriously disturbed person—a cozy evening, with firelight reflecting on the leather books arranged in rows around the walls of the study. Now she just curled miserably in the corner of the couch, glaring at her mother and father. How could she have been born to these cruel, insensitive parents?

Probably, she thought, she had secretly been adopted. Probably her real parents were out there somewhere—kind, normal people: a woman who wore dresses and played bridge; a man who sold insurance and kept nothing but radishes and cucumbers in his crisper.

They had told her, when she asked once, what it was like when she was born. They had said that she looked repulsive at first, and screamed, and peed on the nurse's hand; but later, they said, she had begun to look pretty good, probably the prettiest baby in the nursery. They had also admitted that there were only two babies in the nursery; the other was a Chinese baby named Stanley Wong.

But they could have made all of that up. It suddenly seemed obvious that they *had* made it up. Chinese people wouldn't name a baby Stanley, for Pete's sake.

Somewhere out there, a bridge player and an insurance salesman—kind, compassionate people—

were wishing that they had never given such a sweet baby girl away.

Anastasia sighed and the daydream disappeared. There was this immediate problem to deal with.

"Why not?" she asked, glowering.

"On a purely practical level," said her father, in his purely practical voice, which she hated, "it would be financially impossible. Psychiatrists cost a lot."

"Dad," Anastasia said, filling her voice with as much admiration as she could, considering the fact that he was an insensitive villain, "you're a very famous author. You were nominated for the American Book Award, right? And famous authors make lots of money. That woman who writes Gothic romances is a millionaire. Judith Krantz is probably a millionaire. Judy Blume is probably a millionaire."

"Maybe, Myron," said Mrs. Krupnik, "you should consider changing your name to Judith." She grinned at him and winked. Anastasia cringed. Her parents were so disgusting; they were always doing things like grinning and winking, for Pete's sake.

"I'm a Harvard professor, Anastasia," Dr. Krupnik said. "And on the side, I'm a poet. I'm a pretty successful poet, true. But the fact is that nobody buys poetry. Nobody even *reads* poetry. All they do is give *awards* for poetry. And if I think about that too much I may fall into a serious depression, and then *I'll* need a psychiatrist."

"I remember, Myron," said her mother, "that when you asked me to marry you, you said, 'Katherine, I will never be a rich man.' And I said—" She hesitated. "Well, that's too personal, what I said."

Now *he* grinned and winked. *Gross.*

Anastasia was glad that her mother hadn't gone on to tell what she had said. Probably it was something romantic. Her parents were always doing that, talking about romantic stuff; they were always hugging and kissing, too—even in front of other people. It embarrassed Anastasia just thinking about it. IN FRONT OF OTHER PEOPLE: HUGGING AND KISSING. Talk about gross. Back in the old days, she hadn't even minded.

"Anyway," her father went on, "money isn't the essential thing. It's important, because we don't *have* the money. But even if we did, I'd say no, Anastasia."

"Why?"

"Because you don't *need* a psychiatrist. The people

who need psychiatrists—and there are plenty who do—are people who are emotionally disturbed."

"I've been trying to tell you that I'm emotional—"

"You don't have the slightest symptom of even a minor neurosis. What you do have is an absolutely normal reaction to growing up. When people become thirteen or so, they suddenly realize that their parents are human. Naturally it comes as a shock." Dr. Krupnik began to pick up the evening paper.

"Human? HUMAN!" Anastasia emerged from her curled-up ball and sat up straight. "You call it human to ignore my suffering? How do you know I don't have symptoms of necrosis?"

He chuckled. "Neurosis. *Necrosis* means 'death.' It comes from the Greek."

"Okay, okay; so I'm stupid; so I don't know Greek. And I'm not dead, I'll grant you that. Tell me some symptoms of neurosis. I bet I have all of them."

Dr. Krupnik put the paper down and stroked his beard. He stretched his long legs, in their corduroy pants, toward the fire. "Well," he said. "I'm no expert. I teach English, not Psychology. But here's an example: some very neurotic people have a lot of irrational fears. Some are afraid to be in a crowd. Or some are afraid of wide-open spaces. And of course there are your basic claustrophobics: people who can't even get into an elevator because they're afraid of *confined* places. Or—"

"That's definitely not you, Anastasia," said her mother. "Remember when I lost you at Jordan Marsh, when you were about six? And it turned out you were just riding up and down in the elevator? You hadn't bothered to get off at the fourth floor when I did, because you liked the elevator so much."

"Yeah, I remember," said Anastasia. "That was fun. You got mad, though."

"I really don't think you have any neurotic fears, Anastasia," her father continued.

"Well, I'm scared to death of that old French movie: *Diabolique.* But I don't suppose that would count. Any normal person would be scared of that movie."

"Even me," said her father. "Hey, it's on TV again, real late on Saturday night. You want to stay up and watch it with me?"

Anastasia shuddered. "No. Tell me more psychiatric symptoms."

"Difficulty sleeping?"

"Nope."

"Loss of appetite?"

Anastasia shook her head. "Nope. I said at dinner that I'd lost my appetite, but it was only because of Sam. Actually, after I took my plate to the kitchen, I ate the rest out there."

"Inability to concentrate? That's another symptom."

Anastasia brightened. "I may have that last one. I have a lot of trouble paying attention in math class."

"That doesn't count," said her father. "I mean *real* inability to concentrate, like if you couldn't even follow this conversation."

Mrs. Krupnik yawned. "I can hardly follow this conversation, I'm so sleepy. I'm going to bed in about five minutes."

"Sexual problems," Dr. Krupnik continued. "Are you having sexual problems, Anastasia?"

"*Dad.* Quit being gross."

He chuckled. "Let's see. Delusions. Do you ever think you might be, oh, the Queen of England?"

Anastasia brightened. She made her Queen of England face, raising her eyebrows as high as she could and drawing her mouth into a teeny, pinched position. "I am sometimes teddibly distressed by the conditions in this rawther lower-class home," she said, looking down her nose at her father.

Her mother yawned again. "Me too," she said. "Nobody ever did the dishes tonight. They're still in the sink. It was your turn, Myron; it's Thursday."

He made a face. "I'll do them in the morning," he said. "Anastasia, I'm running out of symptoms. How about: Do you ever think someone is trying to poison you?"

"That's *it!*" said Anastasia. "That's the one I have! Just today, Mom said she was going to make oatmeal for dinner! Talk about poison!"

"Come on, sport. Oatmeal for dinner is disgusting, I'll agree with you there. But did you seriously think that she was going to sneak some ground glass into it?"

"No," admitted Anastasia, grudgingly.

"Well, then. One last symptom. Do you ever hear voices?"

"Sure. I hear yours right now."

"No, I mean phantom voices, inside your head.

Voices that aren't really there, but you hear them anyway."

That was an interesting thought. Anastasia never had. But then she had never really tried to. "Shhh," she said, "let me listen a minute."

Mrs. Krupnik yawned again, as silently as possible. The three of them sat there without speaking, each with their heads cocked to the side, listening.

"Myron," whispered Mrs. Krupnik, "I think I hear a voice!"

"Me too, Dad!" Anastasia said aloud. "I really did hear a voice! I couldn't tell what it was saying, though. It sounded far away."

Her father stood up and put his finger to his mouth. "Shhh," he said, "listen. What *is* that?"

The distant voice had stopped, but now they heard footsteps upstairs. Small footsteps.

"It's Sam," said Mrs. Krupnik. "What's he doing up at this hour?"

The footsteps came to the head of the stairs, and now they could hear the voice loud and clear.

"I threw up!" Sam called cheerfully. "All over my bed!"

"YUCK," said Anastasia.

"It's mostly ketchup!" called the voice. Mrs. Krupnik yawned, stretched, and leaned back in her chair. "Maybe I'll read for a while," she said, and picked up a magazine. "Myron, it's Thursday, remember?"

Dr. Krupnik sighed. "I know," he said. "My turn for cleanup."

"Here," he said, as he got up from his chair. He reached toward the bookcase, took out a book, and handed it to Anastasia. "Read Freud if you want to know about psychiatry."

After her father had gone upstairs to tend to Sam, Anastasia turned to her mother, who was absorbed in a magazine article.

"Dad forgot something important," Anastasia said.

"What's that?"

"Remember that movie we saw on TV? *Sybil?* And Sally Field was this girl who had all these different personalities?"

"Sure," said her mother, "Joanne Woodward was the psychiatrist who cured her. That was a good movie. I wonder why I let you watch it, though.

You were much too young. You were only about eight."

"I was *not* too young," said Anastasia. "I loved that movie. I never forgot it. But it's only just now that I realized I'm like Sally Field. I mean Sybil."

Her mother sighed in exasperation. "Anastasia, you are *not* psychotic!"

"I have all these different personalities seething inside me! I mean really *seething,* Mom!"

Finally her mother slammed the magazine closed and tossed it onto the coffee table. "Anastasia, listen to me. You have lots of different *parts* to your personality. Everybody does. But basically you are a very nice, very bright thirteen-year-old who is experiencing normal difficulty adjusting to adolescence. Did you hear that word 'normal'?"

Anastasia glared at her.

"And part of your personality," her mother went on, "is obnoxious. Frankly, you have been obnoxious lately. And I'm tired, and I wish you would go to bed, because tomorrow's a school day."

Anastasia continued to glare at her. She didn't say anything. Steely eyes, she thought. I am looking at my mother with eyes of steel.

"You want me to be Joanne Woodward, right?" her mother asked. She was really angry now, Anastasia could tell. The steely-eyed look had done it. Sally Field had those same steely eyes when she was being Sybil. "You want me to say wise, comforting, curative things to you? *Right?* Like Joanne Woodward?"

"Yes," said Anastasia with steely dignity. "That would be nice, I think."

"Well, let me tell you something. Joanne Woodward had a script! Someone wrote all her dialogue! And that's the whole blasted trouble with motherhood—there isn't any script!" Mrs. Krupnik was furious. "Now *go to bed!*"

Anastasia stood up with perfect posture, and tilted her nose into the air, with her glasses balanced midway down. "Good night," she said cooly. She nodded haughtily to her mother, who was becoming pretty steely-eyed herself. She left the room, carrying the volume of Freud, and headed up the stairs.

On the second floor, as she headed toward the small staircase that led to her third-floor bedroom, she could hear Sam splashing in the bathtub. Through the open door of Sam's bedroom she could see her father bending over to change Sam's sheets. She caught a glimpse of ketchup and averted her eyes quickly.

Talk about a lower-class environment, Anastasia thought. Queen Elizabeth would *hire* someone to do that.

Anastasia unlaced her hiking boots, dropped them on the floor, and flopped down on her bed. She glanced over at the goldfish bowl, where Frank Goldfish was swimming in slow, lazy circles. Frank never seemed to be emotionally disturbed. Of course, Anastasia had never kept it a secret from Frank that he had been adopted at a very young age.

She looked at the gerbil cage. Both gerbils were busy, rushing around in the shavings, pushing pieces into mounds to make nests. It sure is boring to observe gerbils, Anastasia thought.

She flipped idly through the pages of her father's book. Then she picked up the science project notebook, found her pencil, and began to write.

Science Project

Anastasia Krupnik
Mr. Sherman's Class

On October 13, I acquired two wonderful little gerbils, who are living in a cage in my bedroom. Their names are Romeo and Juliet, and they are very friendly. They seem to like each other a lot. Since they are living in the same cage as man and wife, I expect they will have gerbil babies. My gerbil book says that it takes twenty-five days to make gerbil babies. I think they are already mating, because they act very affectionate to each other, so I will count today as DAY ONE and then I will observe them for twenty-five days and I hope that on DAY 25 their babies will be born.

This will be my Science Project.

Day Three.

My gerbils haven't changed much. They lie in their cage and sleep a lot. They're both overweight, because they eat too much, and they resemble Sonya Isaacson's mother, at least in chubbiness.

In personality, they resemble *my* mother. They're very grouchy.

Day Three Continued.

People who have serious emotional problems sometimes have difficulty doing real good gerbil-observation because they suffer from inability to concentrate. I myself have serious emotional difficulties so I have this problem.

As part of my Science Project I will talk about serious emotional problems. I will tell you what someone named Freud says about this.

The division of the psychical into what is conscious and what is unconscious is the fundamental premise of psycho-analysis; and it alone makes it possible for psycho-analysis to understand the pathological processes in mental life, which are as common as they are important, and to find a place for them in the framework of science.

Anastasia read aloud what she had written. She glanced at the gerbils. They were both asleep in the nests they had built. She looked at Frank Goldfish. He swam in a circle, opening and closing his mouth. She could tell that he was amused.

"Quit being so arrogant, Frank," she said angrily. "Just wait till you're thirteen. *Then* you won't be so well adjusted."

four

"Is it Saturday, Mom?" asked Sam anxiously as he ate his breakfast cereal. "Promise me that it's Saturday?"

"I promise," said Mrs. Krupnik. "It's Saturday. All day."

"Good," said Sam, as he took another bite of Rice Krispies. "I love Saturday. Because on Saturday I don't have to go to nursery school."

Anastasia was sitting on the kitchen floor, lacing up her hiking boots. She'd had to unlace them completely to put them on because she was wearing two pairs of thick wool socks; it was suddenly very cold outside for mid-October. "Why?" she asked her brother. "I thought you loved nursery school. You like those blocks with the letters on them."

But Sam shook his head gloomily. "My friend Nicky takes the blocks and throws them. I'm scared of Nicky. My friend Nicky punches me and kicks me."

"Some friend," said Anastasia, tugging at her boot laces.

"Nicky does *what?*" Mrs. Krupnik put her cup of coffee down on the table and stared at Sam.

"Punches," said Sam. "And kicks."

"Myron, did you hear that?" asked Mrs. Krupnik. "Myron, stop reading the paper for a minute. Did you hear what Sam just said?"

Reluctantly, Dr. Krupnik lowered his newspaper. "Have you read this article about the possibility of a nuclear disaster here in Massachusetts?" he asked.

"No," said Katherine Krupnik. "I have enough problems right here in this house. Did you hear what Sam just told us? There's a child in his nursery school who beats him up!"

"Nicky," said Sam cheerfully. "Nicky punches and kicks. And *bites,* too. Look!" He pulled up the sleeve of his striped jersey. On the side of his arm was a small pink semicircle of teeth marks.

"Myron! Look at this!" Mrs. Krupnik examined Sam's arm with dismay.

Dr. Krupnik adjusted his glasses and took a look. "It didn't break the skin," he said. He began to pick up the newspaper again.

"What is Nicky's full name, Sam?" Mrs. Krupnik asked angrily. She was reaching for the telephone book.

Sam thought about that, wrinkling his forehead as he munched on his cereal. "Big fat ugly Nicky," he said, finally.

Anastasia giggled. "Mom meant *last* name, Sam," she explained. "Like your last name is Krupnik. What's Nicky's last name?"

Sam thought. "Coletti," he said. "Nicky Coletti."

Anastasia stood up and stamped her feet to make sure her boots were just right. "Sounds like Mafia to me," she said. "Definitely underworld. If you call Nicky's mother, Mom, probably thugs will come to the house and break both your legs."

Sam grinned.

Mrs. Krupnik was running her finger down the page of C's in the telephone book. "Cohen," she murmured. "Colby. Coleman—"

Dr. Krupnik put the newspaper down again. "Don't call her, Katherine," he said.

"Is that an order?" asked his wife angrily.

"No, it's a suggestion. Don't you remember what happened when Anastasia was about seven, and she came home one day crying because her friend—What was that little girl's name, Anastasia?"

"Traci," said Anastasia. "It was Traci Beckwith, that little fink."

"Right," said her father. "Traci Beckwith had pushed Anastasia off a swing in the playground, if I remember correctly."

"Yes, she did. I got all this gravel in my knee."

"And you called Mrs. Beckwith, Katherine, remember? You were furious."

"I had every right to be furious. That child could have killed Anastasia. Imagine, pushing a seven-year-old off a swing!"

Dr. Krupnik lit his pipe. "And Mrs. Beckwith, you'll recall, became very aggressive?"

"I had no idea that woman was a criminal lawyer," said Mrs. Krupnik. "But it wouldn't have changed things if I *had* known."

"And she began making countercharges," Dr. Krupnik went on. "She said that Anastasia had taken scissors during art period and had cut the ends off of Traci's pigtails."

"Well," said Anastasia hurriedly, "that was no big deal. She had these very *long* pigtails. And her desk was right in front of mine, so her stupid pigtails were always dangling on my desk and flopping into my finger-painting. There wasn't any need to make a federal case out of it."

"My point," said her father, puffing on his pipe, "is only that before we knew it, the two mothers were talking about lawsuits, and yelling at each other over the phone. But in the meantime, Anastasia and Traci were the best of friends. They were out riding their bikes together."

"I don't see how that relates to Sam," said Mrs. Krupnik grumpily. But she had closed the telephone book. "Who gave that Coletti kid the right to gnaw a whole chunk out of Sam's little arm?"

"Yeah," said Sam mournfully. "A whole big chunk." He gazed at the small pink mark on his arm.

"Why didn't you bite Nicky Coletti back, Sam?" asked Anastasia.

Sam's eyes grew wide. "Nicky Coletti is *big,*" he said. "Nicky Coletti is a *giant.*"

They all stared for a moment at the tiny pink teeth marks.

"Well," said Dr. Krupnik, "I think it's best to let the kids work it out between themselves."

"Maybe so," said Mrs. Krupnik reluctantly. "But I found their name in the book: Coletti, on Woodville Avenue. Just in case I ever need to call."

There was a knock on the kitchen door.

"Oh, no!" cried Anastasia. "That's Sonya and Meredith. We're going to a garage sale on Bennington Street. Oh, rats! They're five minutes early!"

"So what?" asked her mother, puzzled. "Go let them in."

"*Mom,*" said Anastasia, "you're wearing your bathrobe!"

Her mother looked down at her plaid wool bathrobe. "It's clean," she said. "Surely they've seen bathrobes before."

"Mom," said Anastasia hastily, "just do me a big favor, okay? Hide. Go stand in the pantry. It'll only be for a few minutes. And, Dad?"

Her father looked up from the paper. "I'm dressed," he pointed out.

"Hide your pipe. Sonya's father is a doctor. I don't want her to know that you smoke. And, Sam! Quick. Somebody comb Sam's hair, okay? And wipe your face, Sam; there's a Rice Krispie stuck on your chin."

Anastasia's parents and brother all stared at her in astonishment. None of them moved. Dr. Krupnik continued to puff on his pipe. Sam chewed silently on a mouthful of Rice Krispies.

There was another knock at the back door.

Anastasia threw up her arms in disgust. She grabbed her jacket from the doorknob where it was hanging. "All right, then!" she said. "Humiliate me! See if I care! I won't even ask them in!"

She slammed the back door behind her as she went out. "Hi," she said to her friends. "I thought you guys would never get here."

It was much more fun being with her friends than it was being at home with her family, Anastasia thought. Her friends never acted stupid or anything. Tall, slim, pale-blond Meredith Halberg was full of fun; and Sonya Isaacson, chubby and freckled, was good-natured and bookish.

And they knew how to dress. The three of them were all dressed alike, in jeans and hiking boots and jackets. Last week a girl in seventh grade had come to school wearing a jumper and a ruffled blouse, and everyone had hooted and laughed and teased her until she almost cried. Her mother had made her dress that way, the girl explained, because they were going to the airport after school, to meet her grandmother, who was flying in from Chicago.

It was the kind of thing Anastasia's mother might do too. Thank goodness she didn't have a grandmother in Chicago.

"It's really getting cold," said Meredith as the three girls headed down the street. "I hope it snows soon. If it snows before Thanksgiving, my whole family's going skiing over vacation. We always go to this ski lodge in New Hampshire."

"I don't even know how to ski," said Anastasia. "But if I did, I can't imagine going with my family. My parents would act weird. My father would recite poetry about snowfall, and my mother—well, my mother is such a klutz, she'd probably fall all the time. And then she'd laugh. My mom's big on *laughing,* for Pete's sake. It's so embarrassing."

"My mother laughs too," said Meredith. "And she does it with a Danish accent, so it's even worse. But I just pretend that I don't know her. Her *or* my father. My sister and I just take off, at the ski lodge. The only time we have to see our parents is at dinner. And sometimes my sister even eats at a different table."

"How old is your sister?" asked Anastasia. "She's pretty old, isn't she?"

"Kirsten? Seventeen. Why?"

Anastasia stopped in the middle of the sidewalk, her shoulders slumped inside her jacket. "Oh, terrific!" she wailed, in a voice that meant it wasn't terrific at all. "I thought it was only when you were *thirteen* that you felt this way about your family! You mean it lasts till you're seventeen?"

Meredith thought it over. "I don't think it's the same," she said. "Kirsten doesn't even notice our parents. She goes off by herself because she wants to pick up guys when she's skiing."

"That's Stage Two," said Sonya, who had been listening intently. "Stage Two of Adolescence. We're still in Stage One. My father told me that."

"Doctors," scoffed Anastasia. "They always think they know everything."

Sonya shrugged. "He says it's all hormones."

"Hormones schmormones," said Anastasia. "My mother said the same thing. But I think it's a lie. I think grownups got together and made up this hormone theory. I don't even believe in hormones," she added gloomily.

"When my father said that, about the hormones," Sonya went on, grinning, "my brother said he knew a joke. And the beginning of the joke was: How do you make a hormone? But then my father got mad and said, 'None of that at the dinner table!' So I never got to hear the punch line."

"I don't think there's anything funny about hormones, anyway," Meredith said. "I hate the idea that there are all these *things* inside me. What do you suppose they look like? Insects or something?"

"Blecchhh," said Anastasia.

"Here's Bennington Street," said Sonya. "And there's a sign up there in the middle of the block—that must be the garage sale."

They turned the corner and headed toward the large Tudor house with the sign in the driveway.

"You know what?" asked Anastasia. "I told my parents that I wanted to go to a psychiatrist. But they said no. They said I didn't have any problems. Do you believe they said that? *No problems?*"

Sonya and Meredith sighed sympathetically and shook their heads.

"I read in the paper about a girl our age," said Meredith, "who was undergoing psychiatric evaluation at the state hospital."

"How come?" asked Anastasia. "Did her hormones get out of control?"

"She stole fourteen cars," Meredith explained. "And she didn't even have a driver's license. She even stole her own grandfather's car."

They had reached the driveway and turned in toward the garage. Its door was open, and a few people were prowling around through the assorted objects.

Suddenly Meredith started to laugh. "Anastasia," she said, "you're going to go to a psychiatrist whether your parents like it or not!"

She pointed. On the side entrance of the house, a small bronze sign said: CALVIN MATTHIAS, M.D. PSYCHIATRY. PATIENTS' ENTRANCE.

"Oh, I knew that," said Sonya. "Dr. Matthias died—that's why they're having the garage sale."

"How did he die?" asked Anastasia.

"Are you sure you want to know? It's sort of gross," Sonya said. "It wasn't in the paper or anything, but my father told me about it."

"Of *course* we want to know," said Meredith.

"Well," Sonya explained, "a regular patient came in—a man—and they said hello to each other and everything, and then the patient lay down on the couch the way he always did, and Dr. Matthias sat in a chair, the way *he* always did, and the patient started to talk, and he talked for a whole hour until his appointment was over. And Dr. Matthias didn't say anything for the whole hour, but the man didn't notice because Dr. Matthias *never* said anything. And then the patient got up to leave, and went to say goodbye, but Dr. Matthias was dead. He'd been dead the whole hour."

"You mean," Anastasia asked, "the guy had been talking to a dead body for an hour?" It made her feel queasy, just thinking about it.

"That's what the medical examiner said," Sonya explained matter-of-factly. "Apparently he had died of a heart attack, just after he sat down in the chair."

"Gross," said Anastasia. "Maximo grosso."

"Did the guy demand his money back?" Meredith asked.

"I dunno," said Sonya. "I never thought about that. But when my father was telling us about it, at dinner, he said it probably didn't make much difference, because if Dr. Matthias never said anything anyway, so what if he was dead?"

"I'd demand my money back," said Meredith. "I demanded my money back when I found a dead beetle in a bag of popcorn at the movies. It seems like the same thing to me."

"After my father told us about it, my brother said he knew a joke about a psychiatrist. And it started: Once a man went to a psychiatrist and said, 'Doctor, you have to help me, because everything I see reminds me of breasts.'"

"What did the psychiatrist say?" asked Anastasia.

Sonya shrugged. "I don't know. Because my father said, 'None of that at the dinner table.'"

"SONYA!" wailed Anastasia and Meredith together.

"I only know the beginnings of jokes," Sonya said wistfully. "I don't know one single punch line."

"Now listen," said Sonya seriously as they stood in the driveway, "let's make a pact. This time we won't buy junk."

"I *like* junk," giggled Meredith.

"I do too," said Anastasia. "But Sonya's right. I wasted five whole dollars last time. I bought that ashtray shaped like a pair of hands. And I don't even smoke."

"Yeah," Meredith admitted. "And I bought that shower curtain. My mother made me throw it out, because there was mold on it. But it had those neat swans all over it."

"I'm only going to look for books," said Sonya. "Really good books. No trash."

"I suppose I could look for a birthday present for my sister," Meredith mused.

"Does she smoke?" asked Anastasia.

"Yeah. But don't tell my parents."

"For three dollars I'll sell you this ashtray shaped like a pair of hands."

"How about two dollars?" asked Meredith. "I didn't charge you anything for the gerbils, and I gave you their cage and everything, and the book about how to take care of them."

Anastasia pondered that. "That's true," she said. "But don't forget that your mother said that if you didn't get rid of them she was going to put them down the garbage disposal. So I really did you a favor by giving them a good home."

"Well," said Meredith, "let me look through this garage. If I don't find anything, I'll buy the ashtray from you. What are you going to buy?"

"I'm not sure," said Anastasia. "I always have to wait until something sort of, you know, *strikes* me."

Sonya had wandered off, into the garage, and was looking through a large shelf of books. They caught up with her.

"I found *Wuthering Heights,*" she said blissfully. "My very favorite book."

"Don't you already have *Wuthering Heights*?" asked Meredith, who was leaning over a box full of fishing tackle.

"You can never have too many copies of *Wuthering Heights,*" said Sonya, clutching the dusty volume.

"Do you think Kirsten would like a fly-tying kit for her birthday?" asked Meredith. She held up a musty box.

"No," said Anastasia. "She'd like an ashtray shaped like a pair of hands."

"Here, Anastasia!" said Sonya, who was still looking through the bookshelf. She pulled out a thick blue book. "The complete works of Freud! Just the thing for you!"

"I read it the other night," Anastasia said. She moved around to the end of the bookshelf and knelt to examine a box full of kitchen utensils on the garage floor. Suddenly there was a shifting noise; she glanced up and saw Sonya attempting to return the blue book to the crowded shelf. Like dominoes, all the books began to tilt and lean; finally they fell to their sides, one after another. Above Anastasia, at the end of the shelf, where it had been placed as a bookend, something large and cream colored—something very solid-looking—wobbled and fell.

Anastasia jumped aside, but not quickly enough. The object whacked the corner of her forehead—she winced with the sharp pain—and then crashed to the floor.

"Ow," muttered Anastasia. She rubbed her forehead, and could feel a bump starting to rise. "Am I bleeding?"

Sonya examined her. "No," she said. "It's okay, I think. You should put ice on it when you get home. I'm really sorry."

They looked down at the object on the floor. It was the head of a man, a plaster bust of an old-fashioned bearded man with solemn eyes. And no nose. His nose was lying beside him on the floor of the garage.

The price tag taped to the man's head said $4.50.

"Well," sighed Sonya. "There goes *Wuthering Heights.* I guess I just bought myself a noseless man."

Anastasia picked up the nose and held it against

the serious plaster face. "Hello," she said. He stared back at her with blank eyes.

"I kind of like him," she told Sonya. "You know what? I think I'll buy him—then you won't have to, even though you broke him. I think Elmer's glue will reattach his nose."

"Really? You really like him? You're not just saying that because you feel sorry for me?"

Anastasia tucked the man under one arm and headed for the person who was collecting money in the nearby corner. "Nope," she said to Sonya. "It was like I said to Meredith. Something would strike me."

She gave a five-dollar bill to the woman sitting at a card table with a box of change. She pocketed two quarters in return.

"Young lady," said the woman, who had gray hair and large horn-rimmed glasses, "you got a great bargain. You just bought yourself Sigmund Freud."

"Mom? Dad?" called Anastasia as she went in through the back door, clutching Freud under one arm. "I need ice cubes because I got whacked on the forehead."

"And guess what?" she added. "I have a psychiatrist!"

Half an hour later, after an ice-cube treatment, Anastasia's bump had disappeared, leaving only a pinkish bruise. And Freud, after a treatment of Elmer's glue, had his nose back. Anastasia carried him upstairs toward her room.

She found Sam sitting unhappily on the stairs to the third floor. He was sucking his thumb, and his old security blanket was wrapped around his arm. Now that Sam was three, he rarely needed the yellow frayed blanket that had been his constant companion when he was younger. Anastasia knew that something must be terribly wrong.

"Hey, old Sam," she said, "what's the matter?"

He looked at her fearfully. "Don't go up to your room," he said.

"Why not? I have to take my friend Freud up there."

Sam sucked harder on his thumb.

Anastasia knelt beside him. "Were you in my room?" she asked.

He nodded miserably.

"Did you do something bad?"

Tears began to stream down Sam's cheeks. Anastasia set Freud on the step. "Tell me what you did, Sam."

"I broke the gerbils," Sam sobbed.

Anastasia started up the stairs. Behind her, Sam followed, still crying and trying to explain. "I just only reached in to pat them, and I was very very gentle like you told me to be, and they just *broke!* There are a million pieces of gerbil all over the cage!"

Anastasia put Freud on her bed temporarily and then went to the gerbil cage under the window. Sam stood apprehensively behind her.

There was one furry gerbil in its nest in one of corner of the cage; and there was the other furry gerbil in its nest in the other corner. But surrounding each of them were numerous squirming pink creatures.

"Sam!" said Anastasia happily. "They're not broken! They had babies!"

Sam took his thumb out of his mouth and peered around her, into the cage. "Even the father had babies?" he asked.

"Well, I guess I was wrong. Instead of a father and a mother, we had two mothers." She thought briefly about her science project. This was certainly going to complicate her science project.

"They sure had millions of babies," said Sam in an awed voice, looking at them.

"Let me count." Anastasia leaned over the cage and checked the number of babies. "Romeo has four," she announced. "And Juliet has four. So there are eight babies. No, wait—there's one more. Juliet has five. Altogether there are nine. Good grief, we have to think of nine new names."

"Can I name them?" asked Sam. "Because you got to name the first two."

"Sure," said Anastasia. She went to the bed and picked up Freud. She looked around the room, decided on her desk, and placed him there, beside her schoolbooks. Sam squatted by the gerbil cage very intently. Finally he looked up.

"Okay," he said. "I got names."

Anastasia took a pencil and paper to write them down. "What are they?" she asked.

"Happy is one."

"That's a good name. What else? Eight more."

"Sleepy and Dopey and Sneezy and Grumpy and Bashful and Doc."

Anastasia grinned. "Terrific, Sam. But that's only seven. We need two more."

"Snow White," said Sam.

Anastasia wrote it down. "Good," she said. "One more."

Sam beamed. "Prince," he said.

Science Project

Anastasia Krupnik
Mr. Sherman's Class

On October 13, I acquired two wonderful little gerbils, who are living in a cage in my bedroom. Their names are Romeo and Juliet, and they are very friendly. They seem to like each other a lot. Since they are living in the same cage as man and wife, I expect they will have gerbil babies. My gerbil book says that it takes twenty-five days to make gerbil babies. I think they are already mating, because they act very affectionate to each other, so I will count today as DAY ONE and then I will observe them for twenty-five days and I hope that on DAY 25 their babies will be born.

This will be my Science Project.

Day Three.

My gerbils haven't changed much. They lie in their cage and sleep a lot. They're both overweight, because they eat too much, and they resemble Sonya Isaacson's mother, at least in chubbiness.

In personality, they resemble *my* mother. They're very grouchy.

Day Three Continued.

People who have serious emotional problems sometimes have difficulty doing real good gerbil-observation because they suffer from inability to concentrate. I myself have serious emotional difficulties so I have this problem.

As part of my Science Project I will talk about serious emotional problems. I will tell you what someone named Freud says about this.

The division of the psychical into what is conscious and what is unconscious is the fundamental premise of psycho-analysis; and it alone makes it possible for psycho-analysis to understand the pathological processes in mental life, which are as common as they are important, and to find a place for them in the framework of science.

Day Five.

My gerbils gave birth to premature babies. Instead of twenty-five days, it took them only five days to have babies.

Now I have eleven gerbils, and their names are Romeo, Juliet, Happy, Sleepy, Sneezy, Dopey, Grumpy, Bashful, Doc, Snow White, and Prince.

I also have a psychiatrist. His name is Freud. He is dead. But there is no need to be grossed out by that because with some psychiatrists it doesn't seem to matter much if they are alive or dead.

five

Freud," said Anastasia, as she lay on her bed early one evening, her math homework spread out around her, "I really need your advice."

She glanced over at her desk. Freud stared at her with his blank plaster eyes. His nose, she noticed, was a little crooked.

"Would you rather be called Dr. Freud?" she asked politely.

He stared blankly into space.

Anastasia sat up, cross-legged on her unmade, book-strewn bed, and gazed across the room at her psychiatrist. She tilted the lampshade on her bedside lamp so that Freud was illuminated a little better and the shadows across his face were gone.

"Or would you mind if I called you by your first name?" she asked. "I know doctors like to be called 'Doctor'—at least Sonya's father does; he likes to be called 'Dr. Isaacson'—but it seems to me that since it's just the two of us here, and we're in my bedroom, not in an office or anything, that we could be kind of informal."

Freud stared blankly across the room.

On a whim, Anastasia took the blue marking pen that she'd been using for math. She brought Freud's head to her bed where the light was better, and carefully, with the marker, drew blue centers in Freud's plaster eyes. Then, with the tip of a black pen, she drew a dot in the middle of each blue circle.

As an afterthought, she used the fine-tipped black pen at the corners of Freud's mouth, turning the edges of his lips upward a bit. She replaced him on the desk and went back to her bed.

She moved her books aside and lay on her back, her arms crossed behind her head.

"Sigmund?" she said shyly, and glanced over at him. He was looking directly at her, and smiling.

"All riiight," murmured Anastasia. "Now we're in business."

It was November already, and nothing much had changed. Life was boring; her parents were boring; Sam was boring; and the gerbils were the most boring of all. She hadn't even added anything to her science project, she realized guiltily. Probably Norman Berkowitz had completed 25 percent of his computer by now, in November, and Anastasia only had two notebook pages about gerbils.

"Sigmund," she said, "I know that probably I'm supposed to tell you about my childhood and all. But what I really want to talk about is my current problems. Is that okay?"

She looked over. Freud smiled. It was okay, apparently.

She sighed. Where to begin? "My friend Daphne Bellingham," she said. "That's a problem. Daphne used to be my really good friend. Daphne and Sonya and Meredith and I used to do everything together.

"But then Daphne got a crush on this dumb boy—this football player. And now she never wants to hang out with me and Meredith and Sonya anymore. She just hangs out around the school football field, watching dumb practices."

Anastasia frowned. "Why do you think that happened, Sigmund?"

He smiled. If her mother had smiled that way, the smile would have meant: "What do *you* think, Anastasia?"

"*I* think," she went on, "that Daphne has entered Stage Two of Adolescence. The stage where you chase guys."

Anastasia sighed. "I guess I'm not at Stage Two yet. I suppose I'll catch up with her sometime."

An explosion of noise erupted in the gerbil cage. Anastasia glanced over, even though she knew what she would see: the gerbils were fighting again.

"Sigmund," she wailed, "I have TOO MANY gerbils!"

Freud grinned knowingly.

"I know, I know. It's my own fault. And I can't get rid of them. Nobody wants gerbils. I was the fifth person Meredith offered them to. And anyway, I need them for my dumb science project."

She sat up and turned the pages of the calendar on the table beside her bed. It told her what she already knew.

"It's Day Twenty-Five today," she muttered. "This

is the day they were supposed to have babies. Instead, the babies are three weeks old, and the cage smells bad, and they make a lot of noise, and I spend half my allowance on gerbil food."

She noticed that Freud was still smiling, so she got up and turned him around. It wasn't amusing, the gerbil problem.

"I'll see you at my next appointment, Sigmund," she said. "Thanks for the help."

"Anastasia!" her mother's voice came up the stairs.

"What? Come on up!"

"You know I can't do that. I can't come in your room, not as long as—well, you know," her mother said. "I don't want to be in the same room as those two things. You come down here to the second floor. I want to talk to you for a minute."

Those two things my foot, thought Anastasia as she started down the stairs. Would you believe those *eleven* things?

In a million years she couldn't tell her mother that there were now eleven gerbils. Her mother would truly freak out. Anastasia had sworn Sam to secrecy.

She had even vacuumed her own room a couple of times.

She found her mother in the second-floor bathroom, rubbing Sam dry with a big towel after his bath. There were fourteen plastic boats churning around in the bath water as it drained.

"What's up, Mom?" Anastasia asked.

"Look at Sam," her mother said, with a worried frown. "Turn around, Sam. Show Anastasia your behind."

Sam turned around dutifully. On his rear was a bruise.

"That kid Nicky Coletti did that to him," Mrs. Krupnik explained.

"Whacked me with a dump truck," said Sam. "Whammo. During juice time."

"Brush your teeth, Sam," said his mother. Sam climbed onto his special wooden stool and reached for his toothbrush.

"What do you think, Anastasia? I know what your father thinks, that they have to work it out themselves. But I'm beginning to get very angry about this. Give me some productive advice."

"Well, for starters, if I were you, I wouldn't let Sam squeeze his own toothpaste," said Anastasia. "Take a look."

Mrs. Krupnik looked. Sam had squeezed a mountain of Crest onto his little blue toothbrush. "I like my toothpaste to be cheeseburger size," he explained.

His mother sighed.

Sam inserted the mound into his mouth. "Iwahong Anashtashis topuhmy tube ed," he said.

"He wants me to put him to bed," Anastasia translated for her mother.

"Cuzh I godda sheecred fo Anashtashia," he said, through the toothpaste.

"Because he has a secret to tell me," she explained.

"Okay," said her mother. "You tuck him in. But give it some thought, about what I should do, okay?"

"Okay," said Anastasia.

"Gimmea kish?" Sam asked his mother.

She hesitated, and then kissed him good night on his ear, avoiding the toothpaste.

"What's the secret?" asked Anastasia as she tucked Sam, de-toothpasted, into his bed. "Something about your rotten friend Nicky Coletti?"

"No," Sam said, shaking his head. "About the gerbils."

"What about them?"

"I want you to spell them for me," he said. "So that I can write 'gerbil' with blocks, at nursery school."

"Oh, that's no problem. Here." Anastasia got a pencil and paper from Sam's little desk. She wrote "gerbil" on it and showed it to him.

Then she thought for a moment. "Uh-oh," she said. "Sam, you have to be very careful that Mom doesn't see this paper. She doesn't even want to *see* the word 'gerbil.' It might make her freak out."

"Okay," Sam said. "I'll keep it in my pocket."

Anastasia picked up his jeans, which were folded over the back of a chair. "I'm putting it right here, Sam," she told him, "in the pocket of your jeans."

He nodded, and snuggled into his covers. "Tomorrow at school," he said, "I'll write 'gerbil' a million times, with blocks."

He frowned sleepily. "Then," he said in a resigned voice, "probably Nicky Coletti will throw them all at my head."

After she had turned off Sam's light and closed her door, Anastasia went back up to her room. She turned Freud's head back around so that it faced her bed.

"Sigmund," she said, "I have to go talk to my mom in a minute, so this will be a short appointment."

He smiled agreeably.

"I have this problem with my mother," Anastasia grumbled. She looked at her psychiatrist.

"You think that's *funny?*" she asked him angrily.

"Well," she said, after a long silence. "Maybe it *is* sort of funny. My *mother* certainly seems to think it is. She finds it wildly amusing that adolescent people hate their mothers."

Freud smiled benignly from the desk.

"I don't really hate her," Anastasia went on. "But she bugs me. Right now it's bugging me that she wants my advice about a complicated problem. How on earth is a thirteen-year-old person supposed to be able to solve a problem that a thirty-eight-year-old person can't solve?"

She looked quizzically at Freud. "How old are *you?*" she asked.

He smiled.

"Well, okay, I know that's not the sort of question you're supposed to ask your psychiatrist," Anastasia acknowledged.

"I wish you could talk," she sighed. Then she caught sight of the book that was still on the floor beside her bed. Now that she had taken over the cleaning of her room, Anastasia had begun vacuuming *around* things. It didn't make any sense to her, the way her mother did it; her mother picked things up, vacuumed, and then put the things back down. Anastasia just went around them; it seemed more logical.

She flipped through the pages of the book on Freud. The phrase "dependent relations" caught her eye. It sounded appropriate. She was a "dependent," she knew; her father had told her that. He listed her as a "dependent" on his income tax every year.

And she was certainly a "relation." She figured she was her mother's closest relation, except maybe for her father.

"Sigmund," she suggested, "I would like you to tell me something about my relation, Mom, since I am her dependent."

She looked again in the book, at the place where she had seen the phrase "dependent relations."

. . . the derivation of the super-ego from the first object-cathexes of the id, from the Oedipus complex, signifies even more for it. This derivation, as we have already shown, brings it into relation with the phylogenetic acquisitions of the id and makes it a reincarnation of former ego-structures which have left their precipitates behind in the id.

She read it through a second time. She glanced over at Freud. His smile looked, suddenly, a little like a smirk.

You ratfink, Sigmund, she thought. What kind of help is *that?*

Anastasia closed the book, adjusted her glasses, and looked through them down her nose at her psychiatrist. What would Queen Elizabeth say, she wondered, to a psychiatrist who laid a trip on her?

"Your views are interesting," she said to Freud in her Queen Elizabeth voice. "I'll give them some thought, when I find time.

"Right now, though," she added, "I have more important things to deal with."

>< >< ><

She found her parents in the study. Her father, as usual, was reading. Her mother was knitting a sweater. Anastasia made a fervent secret wish that the sweater would not be for her.

She hated her mother's hand-knit sweaters. Everybody she knew wore store-bought sweaters from Sears or Jordan Marsh. But her mother wouldn't buy sweaters; oh no, nothing that ordinary for Mrs. Krupnik. *She* had to knit these horrible sweaters—with cables in them, of all things. Talk about *preppy.* Yuck.

Her father was even wearing one, at this very moment. He didn't even *mind* that he had to wear gross handmade sweaters, with cables. Maybe if she could save up enough money she would someday, for his birthday, buy him a decent Orlon sweater at Sears.

"I was thinking about what you said, Mom," said Anastasia, flopping down on the couch. "And I consulted Freud. Is it okay if I talk about it in front of Dad?"

"Sure," said her mother. "He and I don't agree on

how to deal with Nicky Coletti, but we'd both be interested if you can come up with some great scheme."

Her father put down his paper and lit his pipe. "Does it really help, to consult a plaster psychiatrist?" he asked.

"Sure," said Anastasia. "Freud is very helpful."

"That's fascinating. And you actually asked him about the problem with Sam's friend?"

"*Dad,*" explained Anastasia impatiently, "you don't consult someone like Freud about nursery school problems, not *specifically.* You ask Freud general sorts of questions about human relationships. Like—well, like this evening for example, I was discussing dependent relations with him."

"Dependent relations? You ought to ask him what to do about your Uncle George." He turned to Mrs. Krupnik. "Did I tell you that George wrote and asked me for another loan? He wants to invest in a kiwi-fruit farm."

"Your brother George *is* a kiwi-fruit, if you ask me," said Katherine Krupnik.

"I have enough problems of my own," said Anastasia. "If you want to ask a psychiatrist about Uncle George, you have to buy your own psychiatrist."

"How much did Freud cost?" asked her father.

"Four-fifty."

"When you're through with him, will you sell him to me for a discount?"

Anastasia thought that over. She wasn't sure she'd ever be through with Freud. On the other hand, if he was going to keep coming up with unintelligible responses, like the one about dependent relations, maybe she *should* sell him.

"I'll think about it," she told her father. "In the meantime, I could let you have an ashtray shaped like a pair of hands, real cheap."

"No thanks. I like my old hubcap."

Anastasia cringed. It was just one more embarrassing thing about her father. Once, years ago, he had had a car that he loved. When the car got so old that it couldn't be repaired anymore, he junked it, but kept its hubcaps. He used them for ashtrays. He called them his 1957 Ford Thunderbird Memorial Ashtrays, and there were four of them, in four different rooms of their house. Talk about *gross.* Every time friends came over, Anastasia had to stand in front of the hubcaps, so that her friends wouldn't notice them and ask what they were. Just one more in the long list of humiliations in her life.

"Anyway, about Sam—" she began.

Her mother sat up straight suddenly. "Anastasia," she said, looking at her watch. "It's almost nine o'clock. And it's Tuesday."

"Oh, *Mom,*" she wailed.

"Your night for the dishes. They're in the sink."

"I PUT SAM TO BED. DO I HAVE TO DO ALL THE HOUSEHOLD CHORES?"

"No, but you have to do the dishes on Tuesday and Friday. You were a part of the negotiations when we created that schedule, Anastasia."

"But we had *lasagna* for dinner!"

"You love lasagna."

"Not on *Tuesday!* It makes the plates all yucky! It's practically impossible to clean lasagna plates!"

"Try using detergent for a change," her mother suggested dryly. "I've seen you, the way you wash dishes with just water and no soap."

"Spy," muttered Anastasia.

She got up from the couch, groaning. "I'm so tired," she said. "I ache all over. I may have a wasting disease."

Her father had picked up the newspaper again. Her mother had started in on a whole new cable; she was counting the stitches in her knitting.

"You don't even care," said Anastasia in an astounded voice. "You don't even *care* that I may have a wasting disease!"

Her mother reached for the sheet of knitting instructions. "So do I, sweetheart," she said wearily. "Mine's called motherhood."

"I had a plan," called Anastasia as she plodded down the hall toward the kitchen, "about Nicky Coletti. A truly great plan."

She opened the kitchen door and looked at the lasagna plates in the sink. Worse, she looked at the lasagna casserole, empty and crusted with cheese and tomatoes, on the kitchen table. "But I may never tell you guys about it!" she yelled.

Silence. She could picture them there, in the study, both of them smiling sardonically, just like Sigmund.

The dishes were finally finished. Anastasia put on her pajamas and then rummaged through her top bureau drawer until she found an old jar of hand lotion. She smeared some into her dishpan hands. It really wrecked your skin, using detergent. Twice in the past six months at least, she had used detergent, and both times she had had to use hand lotion afterward.

She still had Freud's head turned backward. She was kind of mad at Freud, and she didn't plan to consult him again tonight.

Instead, she looked guiltily at her science project notebook. She looked guiltily at her gerbil cage. Already she had squirted the room with air freshener today, and it needed it again, all because of those dumb gerbils. The gerbil book said that gerbils didn't smell. But the gerbil book lied.

She yawned, and reread what she had written so far for the Science Project. Last time (twenty days ago, she realized guiltily) she had listed the names of the babies. She couldn't even tell which baby was which. How could you do a scientific study if you didn't know which subject was which?

She examined the small print on her king-sized box of marking pens. NONTOXIC, it said. She should have known that already, since Sam had tasted them all and not died.

Well, okay, that was a scientific thing she could do. Carefully, one at a time, she colored eleven gerbil

Science Project

Anastasia Krupnik
Mr. Sherman's Class

On October 13, I acquired two wonderful little gerbils, who are living in a cage in my bedroom. Their names are Romeo and Juliet, and they are very friendly. They seem to like each other a lot. Since they are living in the same cage as man and wife, I expect they will have gerbil babies. My gerbil book says that it takes twenty-five days to make gerbil babies. I think they are already mating, because they act very affectionate to each other, so I will count today as DAY ONE and then I will observe them for twenty-five days and I hope that on DAY 25 their babies will be born.

This will be my Science Project.

Day Three.

My gerbils haven't changed much. They lie in their cage and sleep a lot. They're both overweight, because they eat too much, and they resemble Sonya Isaacson's mother, at least in chubbiness.

In personality, they resemble *my* mother. They're very grouchy.

Day Three Continued.

People who have serious emotional problems sometimes have difficulty doing real good gerbil-observation because they suffer from inability to concentrate. I myself have serious emotional difficulties so I have this problem.

As part of my Science Project I will talk about serious emotional problems. I will tell you what someone named Freud says about this.

The division of the psychical into what is conscious and what is unconscious is the fundamental premise of psycho-analysis; and it alone makes it possible for psycho-analysis to understand the pathological processes in mental life, which are as common as they are important, and to find a place for them in the framework of science.

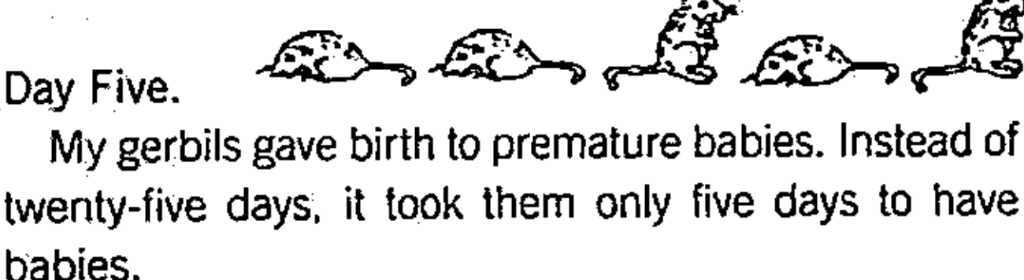

Day Five.

My gerbils gave birth to premature babies. Instead of twenty-five days, it took them only five days to have babies.

Now I have eleven gerbils, and their names are Romeo, Juliet, Happy, Sleepy, Sneezy, Dopey, Grumpy, Bashful, Doc, Snow White, and Prince.

I also have a psychiatrist. His name is Freud. He is dead. But there is no need to be grossed out by that because with some psychiatrists it doesn't seem to matter much if they are alive or dead.

Day Twenty-five.

I have not written anything for a long time because I have felt very tired and it may be that I have a wasting disease. My dependent relations have no sympathy for someone with a wasting disease, I am sorry to say.

Here is what my psychiatrist says about dependent relations:

. . . the derivation of the super-ego from the first object-cathexes of the id, from the Oedipus complex, signifies even more for it. This derivation, as we have already shown, brings it into relation with the phylogenetic acquisitions of the id and makes it a reincarnation of former ego-structures which have left their precipitates behind in the id.

To identify my gerbils scientifically, I have colored their heads.

RED — ROMEO
BLUE — JULIET
YELLOW — HAPPY
GREEN — SNEEZY
ORANGE — BASHFUL
PURPLE — DOC
BROWN — GRUMPY
BLACK — SLEEPY
PINK — DOPEY
TURQUOISE — SNOW WHITE
WHITE — PRINCE

This will make it easier for me to know who is who, in case one of them has babies or something.

To identify my psychiatrist, I have put a large MAGENTA spot on his head. (There is, of course, no chance that my psychiatrist will have babies.)

Anastasia looked into the gerbil cage at the little rainbow-colored heads, burrowing into their nests to go to sleep. Then she looked back at what she had written. Despair overwhelmed her.

In case one of them has babies? She hadn't thought of the possibility before. How old did gerbils have to be, before they had babies? If one of them had, say, four babies, then she would have fifteen gerbils instead of eleven. But what if *two* of them had babies? *Nineteen* gerbils. What if—she could hardly bear to think the thought—all eleven of them had babies? How many gerbils would that make?

Surely some of them were boy gerbils. She thought, suddenly, about a boy in the eighth grade, Kevin Burke, who was one of six brothers. Some families had all boys. Maybe all her baby gerbils were boys.

But she had a horrible suspicion that they weren't.

"Sigmund," she said to her psychiatrist as she climbed into bed, "I may have some problems coming up—problems that no psychiatrist has ever dealt with before."

six

"I've forgiven you guys," announced Anastasia to her parents the next evening, "so I'm going to tell you the plan."

"Forgiven us for what?" asked her mother.

Her mother was standing at the kitchen sink doing the dishes. Anastasia had her homework spread out on the kitchen table. Her room was beginning to smell so bad that she didn't like to do her homework there anymore. She was even worried about Frank Goldfish, though he didn't appear to have a nose.

Freud had a nose, though it was crooked, but she wasn't worried about Freud because his nose was plaster.

"For making me do the dishes last night."

Her father looked up. He had spread newspapers on the kitchen floor and lined up all his shoes on them. He was about to start polishing them. "It was Tuesday," he said. "Tuesday is *your night,* Anastasia."

"Well," Anastasia muttered, "I didn't feel like doing the dishes last night."

Her mother turned around. "Nobody ever feels like doing dishes. *I* never do. Dishes are just something you have to do every night whether you feel like it or not. Dishes are the same as laundry, or going to the dentist, or—"

"—or polishing shoes," said Dr. Krupnik, looking up again.

"Right," said Katherine Krupnik. "Just something you have to do, so you do it without even thinking about whether you *want* to do it."

Anastasia poured some salt into the palm of her hand, and tasted it. "Well," she said, finally, "everyone else in the whole world has a dishwasher."

Her father picked up one of the sheets of newspaper that he had on the floor. "Look," he said, and pointed to a photograph in the paper.

Anastasia looked. It was a picture of a long line

of people wearing ragged clothes, walking barefoot along a dirt road. "Lebanese refugees flee their war-torn city," the caption began.

"So?" she asked.

"So," her father said, and put the paper back down on the floor. "They don't have dishwashers."

"How do you know? It doesn't say, 'Lebanese refugees, who do not have dishwashers —'"

Her father snorted and began polishing one shoe very vigorously, as if he wanted to murder it.

"Anastasia," asked her mother, "do you argue about everything that way with your teachers at school?"

Anastasia poked at the salt in her hand. "No," she admitted. "Only with you guys."

"Well, I wish you'd cut it out. It's very irritating. I also wish you'd tell us about your plan. I'm really fed up with big fat ugly Nicky Coletti, and if you have an idea, I'd like to hear it."

Anastasia brightened. "I do!" she said. "Listen, Mom, what you do is this. You call Mrs. Coletti and—"

Her mother interrupted. "Dad already said he thinks that's not a good idea."

"No, no, you don't call and yell at her. Call and be very polite. Ooze with sweetness. You can do that, Mom. I've *heard* you ooze with sweetness. You're really good at it."

Her mother picked up some clean plates and took them to the cupboard. "When did I? I *never* ooze with sweetness. Do I, Myron?"

He frowned, holding a shoe in one hand. "Well, I have to admit that you do occasionally. Every year, at that faculty wives luncheon, you ooze a bit."

"And when that guy comes to the door selling brooms made by blind people, Mom. You always ooze with sweetness at him."

"Well," muttered Mrs. Krupnik, "I hate that luncheon. And as for the guy selling brooms, I used to *buy* those brooms. I really thought it was terrific that blind people could earn money by making brooms. And then one time I discovered a little sticker on one of those brooms; it said 'Made in Taiwan.' That really made me mad. So I figured I had a choice: I could either whack him over the head with a broom, or I could be sickeningly sweet. You're right, I guess; I do ooze with sweetness when he comes around."

"So," said Anastasia. "Call Mrs. Coletti. Call her

tonight, in fact. Be nauseatingly nice. And invite her to bring Nicky over to play some afternoon."

"Why? Why on earth would I do that to Sam? He has to suffer enough in nursery school."

"Mom," explained Anastasia patiently. "Here's the plan. Make sure that you invite Mrs. Coletti, too, so that she doesn't just drop Nicky off. You want her to stay, so that she can *see* Nicky beating up on poor Sam. She'll be a witness, and she won't think you're just making it up."

"Katherine," said Dr. Krupnik, rubbing one shoe with a brush, "it might work. It sounds good."

"I'll be darned. Anastasia, sometimes you're a genius." Mrs. Krupnik put the last pot away, hung up the dishtowel, and went to the phone. "Listen to me, you guys, while I ooze with sweetness."

"Fifteen minutes," said Mrs. Krupnik. "They should be here in about fifteen minutes."

"I'm going to hide," whimpered Sam. "I'm going to hide in a closet."

It was Saturday afternoon, and Mrs. Coletti was bringing Nicky to play.

"Sam," Anastasia reminded him. "Mom and I

are here. And Nicky's mother will be here, too. We'll protect you, we promise. And remember why they're coming? So Mrs. Coletti will *see* Nicky beating you up. Remember it's all a secret plan?"

Sam nodded, but his eyes were wide. "Yeah," he whispered. "A secret plan."

Mrs. Krupnik arranged cookies on a plate. The teakettle was on, and she had teacups on a tray. Little glasses of juice were ready for Sam and Nicky.

"Sam," his mother suggested, "why don't you bring your oatmeal-box train down to the living room, so you and Nicky can play with it there while the mothers have tea?"

"Okay," Sam said, and trotted off. In a minute Anastasia and her mother could hear the train thumping down the front stairs: fourteen oatmeal boxes attached to each other in a line, with the bright red caboose at the end. The train was Sam's very favorite toy.

The doorbell rang. Sam scurried into the kitchen and stood behind his mother, clutching her skirt. Mrs. Krupnik had changed out of her usual jeans for the Colettis' visit.

"Sam, sweetie," said his mother, "I can't answer the door if you're grabbing me that way."

Reluctantly, Sam let go. Anastasia took his hand, and the three of them went to the front door.

The woman standing there was small and ordinary-looking. "Hello," she said, "I'm Shirley Coletti."

Mrs. Krupnik, oozing with sweetness, ushered her into the house. Behind Mrs. Coletti stood somebody about Sam's size, bundled into a red snowsuit.

"And this must be Nicky," oozed Mrs. Krupnik. "Let me take your coat, Shirley. Anastasia, can you get Nicky's snowsuit?"

Anastasia knelt on the hall floor in front of Nicky Coletti, who looked at her suspiciously with big, dark, long-lashed eyes.

"Lookit the train," said Nicky, peering through the door to the living room. "I wanna play with the train."

"It's *my* train," said Sam. Then he added, reluctantly, "But you can play with it."

Anastasia unzipped Nicky's snowsuit. Her mother had taken Mrs. Coletti into the living room.

She eased the top of the snowsuit down over Nicky's firm little shoulders. She lifted Nicky into a chair and began to maneuver the thick snowsuit legs over Nicky's shoes—Nicky's black patent leather shoes.

That's weird, thought Anastasia. Black patent leather shoes?

Finally she pulled the entire snowsuit off, revealing Nicky's two bare, sturdy legs and a short plaid dress that was hiked up in back, exposing ruffled underpants.

"I'm gonna get that train," announced Nicky. She jumped down from the chair and ran into the living room.

"Sam," said Anastasia in astonishment to Sam, who was hiding in a dark corner of the hall, "Nicky Coletti is a *girl!*"

"Yeah," said Sam. "Big fat ugly Nicky Coletti."

Anastasia took Sam's hand and went into the living room. Her mother was pouring tea for Mrs. Coletti, who was talking nonstop. Nicky was on her hands and knees, pushing the train around the room.

"You got stuck with one of these big old houses, I see," Mrs. Coletti was saying. "I'm lucky; I've got a raised ranch. I've got your four-bedroom, family room, two-and-a-half baths."

"Rrrrrrrrrr," said Nicky in a loud voice, "train wreck, coming up." She was aiming the train for the coffee table. Anastasia cringed and waited for Mrs. Coletti to tell Nicky not to smash the train into the table.

Crash. The table remained intact, though the teacups rattled. But Sam's engine was dented, and the little smokestack fell off.

Mrs. Coletti glanced down. "You shouldn't get those cheap cardboard toys," she said. "I always get Nicky the real sturdy toys: your Playskool and your Tonka."

"Rrrrrrrr," roared Nicky. She took the plate of cookies, tilted it, and emptied it into one of the train cars. Then she headed for the dining room with Sam's train. "Train wreck number two!" she bellowed, and they heard a crash, and the sound of cookies hitting the floor.

Mrs. Krupnik took a deep breath. "More tea, Shirley?" she asked politely.

Sam was sitting beside Anastasia on the couch, listening intently to the noise in the dining room. His chin was puckered, as if he might cry.

"In a new house, like mine," Mrs. Coletti went

on, "you don't get all the dust like you have here. Of course you get your modern heating system. See this?" She reached behind her and ran one finger over the top of the radiator. "With your modern heating system you don't get any of this dust."

Mrs. Krupnik smiled a tight-lipped smile and sipped her tea. "We wanted an older house," she said, "because of the space. This house has room for me to have a studio here, so that I can work at home."

"Oh, you *work?*"

Mrs. Krupnik nodded.

"My mother's an illustrator," Anastasia said. "She does the illustrations for books."

"I'm lucky," said Shirley Coletti smugly. "I never had to work."

"Mom doesn't *have* to work," said Anastasia. "She works because she's good at it. She likes to work."

"I have a real artistic sister," said Shirley Coletti, pouring herself some more tea. "She does her own Christmas cards every year? Last year she did Santa Claus holding a martini glass. You know, you could tell, because it had an olive in it? Then inside it said, ' 'Tis the season to be jolly, Ho Ho Ho.'"

Mrs. Krupnik smiled politely. The dining room

was quiet. They could hear Nicky's "rrrrrr" from some distance; apparently Nicky had headed toward the kitchen.

"Anastasia," her mother said, "maybe you could go and check—"

"Maybe it didn't say 'jolly.' I think it said ' 'Tis the season to be *merry.*' They were real cute, anyway," said Shirley Coletti.

There was a terrible crash from the kitchen. Anastasia jumped up.

"Nicole Marie Coletti!" yelled her mother. "Whatever you're doing, cut it out! Or I'll whip the living daylights out of you!"

The kitchen was empty when Anastasia reached it. But Sam's train was there, its red caboose flattened. Nicky had apparently stood on the caboose to reach the shelf where the cookie jar was. There were cookies everywhere, and the fat blue pottery cookie jar was in shattered pieces on the floor.

Sadly, Anastasia picked up the pieces and dropped them into the wastebasket. Sam appeared in the kitchen doorway.

"My train," he whimpered.

Anastasia put her arm around him. "Mom and I

will try to fix it after that brat leaves," she said. "Right now we'd better find her."

There was a trail of cookie crumbs on the back stairs. They followed it, and found Nicky in the master bedroom. She was spraying herself with Mrs. Krupnik's perfume. She was wearing Mrs. Krupnik's best high-heeled shoes.

Anastasia reached for the perfume bottle, to take it away from Nicky. Nicky bit her on the arm.

"OW!" said Anastasia.

"I *told* you Nicky Coletti bites," said Sam grimly.

Anastasia wrestled Nicky to the floor, took away the perfume, and removed her mother's shoes. Nicky darted away in her stocking feet and disappeared.

Anastasia sighed, picked up Nicky's little patent leather shoes, rubbed the aching bite mark on her arm, and went in pursuit.

The bathroom was empty, but the toilet paper had been unwound and strewn around the floor. A tube of bright green Prell shampoo had been squeezed into the bathtub.

"She's really fast," said Anastasia. "Where do you suppose she went?" She headed toward Sam's bedroom, with Sam trotting behind her.

"My nursery school teacher says that Nicky Coletti is faster than a speeding bullet," said Sam.

His bedroom was ominously quiet. They stood in the doorway, looking in; Sam's finger-paints had been opened, and his bedspread was smeared with blue and green paint.

Suddenly, Nicky appeared, jumping up from her hiding place behind the closet door. She took aim and threw a Matchbox car in their direction. Anastasia shielded Sam, and the missile caught her on the shoulder as it whizzed past.

"OW!" she said again. She grabbed for Nicky, caught her as she dashed by, and pinioned her arms to her sides. Nicky kicked her in the shins.

"I *told* you Nicky Coletti kicks," murmured Sam.

"Nicky," said Anastasia, holding the little girl tightly by the shoulders, "go downstairs. Your mother wants you."

Pouting, Nicky shook herself loose and headed down the front stairs toward the living room. Anastasia followed, rubbing her wounds.

"There you are, Nicky, you little devil," said Shirley Coletti. "If you broke anything, I'm going to tell your daddy to whip you when we get home." She turned back to Anastasia's mother. "So, as I was saying, with your wall-to-wall, like I have, you don't have your problem with trying to keep these old floors clean."

Nicky had sauntered away.

"She's headed for your studio, Mom," said Sam loudly. "And she's already wrecked every other room, almost."

Mrs. Krupnik leaped to her feet and took off after Nicky.

"That Nicky," said Shirley Coletti, smiling at Anastasia. "She's your basic hyperactive? The doctor says that your hyperactives are smarter than other children, did you know that?"

Mrs. Krupnik returned with Nicky, kicking and whining, under one arm. She deposited her unceremoniously in Mrs. Coletti's lap. Nicky curled up, leaned against her mother, and looked slyly at Anastasia.

Mrs. Coletti sniffed. "You found yourself some perfume, didn't you, Nicky? You're a real little lady. Is that one of your Avon products?" she asked Mrs. Krupnik.

"No. It's called Je Reviens," said Katherine Krupnik in an ominous voice.

"French, huh? That's real la-di-da. You know Avon has some real good scents, your florals? And they're not as expensive as your French," said Shirley Coletti.

"Anastasia," said Mrs. Krupnik, "why don't you get Mrs. Coletti's coat? And Nicky's snowsuit?"

"I'll do that," said Anastasia.

Myron Krupnik came through the back door and brushed at the shoulders of his heavy jacket. "It's starting to snow," he announced. "I got the snow tires put on just in time."

His wife was vacuuming cookie crumbs from the kitchen floor. "Move," she said to him. "You're in my way."

Anastasia looked over from the sink, where she was washing the teacups. "Hi, Dad," she said wearily.

"How's it going, old Sam?" asked Dr. Krupnik cheerfully, and leaned over to pick up Sam, who was kneeling on the floor trying to unsquash his red caboose. "Want to feel some snowflakes?"

Sam burst into tears. "Put me down," he wailed.

"Well," said Anastasia's father, depositing Sam back on the floor, "there's nothing like a warm, hearty welcome to make a man feel terrific."

Everyone glared at him.

"I have a feeling," he said slowly, "that the tea party did not go well."

"Where were you?" asked Mrs. Krupnik. "You said you'd be here."

"I got held up at the gas station. Everybody was waiting in line to have their snow tires put on. Why? You didn't need me, did you? To entertain one woman and one little boy?"

"Girl," said Sam.

"Girl," said Anastasia.

"Girl," said Mrs. Krupnik. "One obnoxious, pretentious, irritating woman, and one horrendous, horrible—"

"Hyperactive—" said Anastasia.

"Hyperactive brat. *Yes,* we needed you. Talk about a rat deserting a sinking ship!"

Dr. Krupnik hung his jacket on a hook in the back hall. "Sam, would you get your old dad a beer, please?" he asked.

Sam went to the refrigerator.

"Now tell me all about it, Katherine," Anastasia's father said.

"I'm going upstairs," said Anastasia. "I don't want to hear about it."

"Can I come with you?" asked Sam.

"Sure."

They trudged up the stairs, over the cookie crumbs, past Sam's paint-spattered room and the master bedroom, which still reeked of Je Reviens perfume.

"I don't know which is worse," said Anastasia. "A room filled with French perfume or a room filled with gerbil smell." They headed up the stairs to Anastasia's third-floor room.

"A room with Nicky Coletti in it; *that's* the worst," said Sam.

"Right. Oh, NO!" Anastasia stood in the doorway of her bedroom, looking in. "She was up here, too!"

Anastasia's marking pens were lying all over the floor, with their caps off. There was a wavy line of orange on the wallpaper near her bed; and Freud had a blue spot on the tip of his crooked nose.

She dashed to her goldfish bowl. "Frank? Are you okay, Frank?"

Frank opened and closed his mouth solemnly. He looked all right, but he wasn't his usual cheerful self.

"He's traumatized," Anastasia said. "He's stunned."

"Anastasia," said Sam in a frightened voice. "Look." He was on his knees beside the gerbil cage.

She looked. The top of the cage was unlatched and open, and the gerbil cage was empty.

Science Project

Anastasia Krupnik
Mr. Sherman's Class

On October 13, I acquired two wonderful little gerbils, who are living in a cage in my bedroom. Their names are Romeo and Juliet, and they are very friendly. They seem to like each other a lot. Since they are living in the same cage as man and wife, I expect they will have gerbil babies. My gerbil book says that it takes twenty-five days to make gerbil babies. I think they are already mating, because they act very affectionate to each other, so I will count today as DAY ONE and then I will observe them for twenty-five days and I hope that on DAY 25 their babies will be born.

This will be my Science Project.

Day Three.

My gerbils haven't changed much. They lie in their cage and sleep a lot. They're both overweight, because they eat too much, and they resemble Sonya Isaacson's mother, at least in chubbiness.

In personality, they resemble *my* mother. They're very grouchy.

Day Three Continued.

People who have serious emotional problems sometimes have difficulty doing real good gerbil-observation because they suffer from inability to concentrate. I myself have serious emotional difficulties so I have this problem.

As part of my Science Project I will talk about serious emotional problems. I will tell you what someone named Freud says about this.

The division of the psychical into what is conscious and what is unconscious is the fundamental premise of psycho-analysis; and it alone makes it possible for psycho-analysis to understand the pathological processes in mental life, which are as common as they are important, and to find a place for them in the framework of science.

Day Five.

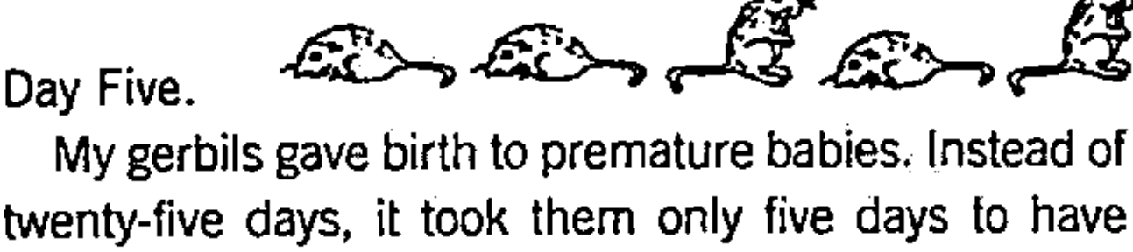

My gerbils gave birth to premature babies. Instead of twenty-five days, it took them only five days to have babies.

Now I have eleven gerbils, and their names are Romeo, Juliet, Happy, Sleepy, Sneezy, Dopey, Grumpy, Bashful, Doc, Snow White, and Prince.

I also have a psychiatrist. His name is Freud. He is dead. But there is no need to be grossed out by that because with some psychiatrists it doesn't seem to matter much if they are alive or dead.

Day Twenty-five.

I have not written anything for a long time because I have felt very tired and it may be that I have a wasting disease. My dependent relations have no sympathy for someone with a wasting disease, I am sorry to say.

Here is what my psychiatrist says about dependent relations:

. . . the derivation of the super-ego from the first object-cathexes of the id, from the Oedipus complex, signifies even more for it. This derivation, as we have already shown, brings it into relation with the phylogenetic acquisitions of the id and makes it a reincarnation of former ego-structures which have left their precipitates behind in the id.

To identify my gerbils scientifically, I have colored their heads.

RED — ROMEO	BROWN — GRUMPY
BLUE — JULIET	BLACK — SLEEPY
YELLOW — HAPPY	PINK — DOPEY
GREEN — SNEEZY	TURQUOISE — SNOW WHITE
ORANGE — BASHFUL	WHITE — PRINCE
PURPLE — DOC	

This will make it easier for me to know who is who, in case one of them has babies or something.

To identify my psychiatrist, I have put a large MAGENTA spot on his head. (There is, of course, no chance that my psychiatrist will have babies.)

Day Twenty-nine.

My gerbils have disappeared.

My gerbil book says this about disappeared gerbils: "If, in the process of escaping, the gerbils have been frightened, it is best to just sit very still in the middle of the floor until the gerbils come out of hiding on their own."

But my scientific assistant, Sam, and I sat very still in the middle of the floor for one hour, and my scientific assistant fell sound asleep while we waited. But the gerbils never appeared.

I think that by now there are eleven gerbils loose all over the house. And if my mother sees even ONE of them she is likely to have a nervous breakdown.

My mother doesn't even know I HAVE eleven gerbils.

And my psychiatrist is no help at all. He has his *own* problems: a villain has painted his nose blue.

seven

"Myron," said Mrs. Krupnik at dinner one night a month later, "I think I should make an appointment with the eye doctor. I think I need glasses."

"Really? I'm surprised. Your vision has always been perfect. I've always thought it was a shame that Anastasia inherited my astigmatism instead of your perfect vision."

"Don't feel bad, Dad," said Anastasia. "I don't mind wearing glasses. I used to think that I wanted contact lenses when I got older. But now I've decided that glasses make me look scholarly. I *like* looking scholarly."

Mrs. Krupnik, at the end of the table, held up a piece of chicken on her fork. She peered at it thoughtfully. "I can *see* all right. This piece of chicken is perfectly clear."

"How about across the room?" asked Anastasia. "If I take my glasses off, I can't tell if that painting on the wall is a landscape or a still life."

Her mother looked across the dining room at the painting. "I can see that just fine," she said.

"Then why do you think you need glasses?"

"It's strange. I've been noticing it for several weeks. Sometimes, out of the corner of my eye—I guess it's my peripheral vision—I see something move. It's just an instantaneous sensation, that something is moving very quickly. Then when I turn to look, nothing is there."

"It could be migraine," said Dr. Krupnik. "Migraine does that to people sometimes."

"It could be Dopey," said Sam. Anastasia glared at him.

His mother laughed. "It *is* sort of dopey, Sam. But I guess I'd better have my eyes tested."

"Sam," said Anastasia later, privately, "remember that you shouldn't mention the gerbils in front of Mom."

"I know," sighed Sam. "I forgot. But it *is* Dopey

she sees, I'm sure of it. Or maybe Grumpy, or Doc, or Romeo."

"Or Sleepy. We don't have Sleepy back yet, either."

"Yeah. Dumb old Sleepy."

There were still five gerbils missing. It had been a frustrating month.

They had found Snow White first, the day after Nicky Coletti's visit. Snow White had holed up in a sneaker in Anastasia's closet. She had poked her head up curiously when Anastasia reached into the closet for a sweater, and had been caught.

Two days later Sam had found Bashful in the coal car of his train.

Two weeks ago, Anastasia had vacuumed up Sneezy when she was cleaning her room. It happened so quickly she couldn't stop it; he was under her bed, and he got sucked right in. Frantically she opened the vacuum cleaner, and there he was, wrapped in a layer of dust. She had thought he was dead. But while she was looking around for a small coffin, he opened his eyes suddenly. If she hadn't grabbed him, he would have taken off again.

The day after that, Sam had come across Juliet sitting right in the middle of the kitchen floor, eating a

Rice Krispie. Fortunately, his mother had not been in the kitchen at the time.

Happy had finally surfaced last week, in a pile of dirty clothes that Anastasia had been carrying down from her room. He had eaten a hole in the sleeve of her favorite T-shirt.

And she had discovered Prince only yesterday, sitting in the dirt of a potted plant in the living room, munching on a leaf of her mother's favorite begonia.

But there were still five gerbils missing. Anastasia wondered if they had starved to death by now. She realized guiltily that she didn't really care if they had.

And her psychiatrist was no help at all. He continued to smile serenely, even when Anastasia was at the peak of despair. It was as if Freud didn't even *care* about the missing gerbils.

Freud would certainly have to care if Mrs. Krupnik had a total nervous breakdown; and Mrs. Krupnik would certainly have a total nervous breakdown if she knew there were five gerbils loose in her house.

"Mom," asked Anastasia during dessert, "are you in any particular part of the house when you have this problem with your eyes?"

Her mother thought. "I hadn't considered that. I remember that it's happened in the studio. Several times in the studio. I've been working, and then I'd see this—this *movement*—over to the side."

"It must be the light in there, Katherine," said Dr. Krupnik. "The light's very bright in there, particularly this time of year when there are no leaves on the trees. I think it's migraine. Bright light affects migraine."

"What day is today?" asked Anastasia. "Wednesday?"

"Yes," said her father. "Mom's turn for the dishes."

"While you're doing the dishes, Mom, could I use your studio? I want to do some drawings for my science project."

Mrs. Krupnik cringed. "As long as you don't use live models, Anastasia. I will *not* have those two things in my studio."

"I will definitely not take any live creatures into your studio, Mom," she promised truthfully.

Sam grinned. "Dopey," he murmured under his breath. "I think it's Dopey."

>< >< ><

But it wasn't Dopey. It was Romeo and Doc. When Anastasia turned on the studio light, she saw them, sitting side by side on the table, gnawing on a 4-H pencil. She recognized their red and purple heads. They looked up, startled by the light, and turned to scamper away. But Anastasia was too quick for them. She grabbed a basket of fruit that her mother had been using as a model for a still life, dumped three pears and a banana on the floor, and overturned the basket on top of the gerbils. They were caught.

With both gerbils tightly restrained in one hand, she replaced the fruit in the basket, turned off the light, and left the studio. In the hall, she met her father coming out of his study.

"That was fast," he said. "Are you all finished already?"

Anastasia held her handful of gerbils behind her back.

"I am for now," she said.

He hesitated. "Anastasia, I need to speak to you privately," he said. "Do you have a few minutes?"

"Sure," she told him, with her hand still uncomfortably behind her back. All of a sudden, her hand was wet. One of the gerbils had peed in her hand. "But I have to go upstairs for a minute first."

"I'm going to go get some coffee," her father said. "I'll meet you in the study."

Anastasia took the gerbils to her room and put them into the cage. She counted. Eight down, and three to go.

She went to the bathroom to wash her hands. Gerbil pee, for Pete's sake, she thought. The things I have to go through. Talk about disgusting.

Sam wandered by the bathroom and looked in. "Did you find him?" he asked. "Was it Dopey?"

"It was Romeo and Doc," she told him. "And Romeo was disgusting. He has no self-control."

"So, Dad, what's up?" asked Anastasia. "What do you want to talk to me about?"

He looked uncomfortable. "I find this very embarrassing," he said.

Anastasia was astonished. "You're not going to talk about the facts of life, are you, for Pete's sake? You and Mom already did that, *years* ago!"

He laughed, and lit his pipe. "No. This is a problem I have, and I don't want your mother to know about it."

"But you and Mom don't have any secrets from each other!"

"Normally we don't," he admitted. "But you know your mother's still upset about that Coletti child. I just hate to add another problem to her list, especially one as bizarre as this. This one would *really* blow her mind."

He has a mistress, Anastasia thought suddenly. My father has a mistress. He's fallen in love with one of his students: a sweet young thing with big eyes and dangly earrings, and they're planning to run off together and be vegetarians, and maybe join a weird religion, and probably he's going to take the stereo with him too.

"Well, it might upset me, too!" she said angrily. "Didn't you ever think of *that?*"

"There was this movie a while back—I'm sure you saw it," her father said.

Anastasia tried to think of a movie in which a middle-aged man ran off with a young vegetarian.

"*An Unmarried Woman*?" she asked suspiciously.

"No," he said. "It was called *Poltergeist.*"

He doesn't have a mistress, Anastasia thought. I knew it couldn't be that. Not my good old dad. She relaxed. "I hated *Poltergeist,*" she said.

"Me too. And I've never believed in that stuff—ghosts that move objects around and break things."

"Idiotic," said Anastasia.

"Right. That's what I always thought. But, Anastasia, I think I have one."

"A *ghost?*"

Her father nodded miserably. "A poltergeist. Right here in my study."

Anastasia looked around the study, her favorite room in the whole house besides her own bedroom—and lately she'd begun to hate her bedroom, because it smelled like gerbils. The study was lined with bookcases filled with books. There was the fireplace, her father's big desk, the soft couch with its piles of bright-colored pillows, her mother's paintings on the walls.

"*Here?*" she asked in amazement.

He sucked on his pipe, looked around, and shuddered. "I know. It sounds ridiculous. But lately things have been moving, just the way they did in that movie. Earlier this evening, I was sitting at my desk correcting some papers, and suddenly I heard a metallic sort of clunk."

"A clunk?"

"Exactly. And when I looked up, my hubcap ashtray was still vibrating. It had jumped up and down."

They both stared at the hubcap.

"And it's happened before. The hubcap jumps, but when I look at it, there's nobody there. Sometimes I've thought that Sam must be hiding behind the couch, playing tricks. But he isn't. There's never anybody there.

"And once," he went on, "I saw a book move. Up there, in the bookcase. Just a fraction of an inch. But I *saw* it, Anastasia. It jumped out of the bookcase a fraction of an inch. Look: I left it that way. See how that one book is sticking out farther than the others?" He pointed.

Anastasia looked, and began to grin. "It's Dopey," she said.

"Don't say that," her father said. "It's Hemingway."

Out of the corner of her eye, Anastasia saw a sudden, swift darting movement between the desk and the couch.

"Dad," she whispered, "sit very, very still."

He froze.

Moving silently, inch by inch, Anastasia approached Dopey, who was hunched over, hiding behind the leg of the couch. With a quick thrust of her hand, she grabbed him. She held him up, tail dangling. "There's your poltergeist, Dad!"

Her father adjusted his glasses and looked carefully at the squirming Dopey.

"A gerbil," he said. "I thought you had your two gerbils in your room, Anastasia. And why is his head pink?"

Anastasia sighed. "Dad," she said, "I'm going to tell you something. But you must *promise* not to tell Mom."

"Well, you're right, Anastasia," her father said, emptying the tobacco from his pipe into his hubcap, "we certainly mustn't tell your mother. How many did you say are still missing?"

"Now that I've caught Dopey, two more."

The door to the study opened a few inches. "Don't

come in, Mom," said Anastasia hastily, holding Dopey behind her. "Dad and I are having a private conversation."

"It's me," said Sam, poking his head around the door. "Grumpy and Sleepy!"

"Everybody's grumpy when they're sleepy, Sam," said his father. "Come on, I'll take you up to bed."

"No, look!" Then he hesitated. "Can I show Dad?"

Anastasia nodded, chuckling.

Sam held up his two fists, with a tail dangling from each. "In my slippers!" he said. "They were in my bedroom slippers!"

Science Project

Anastasia Krupnik
Mr. Sherman's Class

On October 13, I acquired two wonderful little gerbils, who are living in a cage in my bedroom. Their names are Romeo and Juliet, and they are very friendly. They seem to like each other a lot. Since they are living in the same cage as man and wife, I expect they will have gerbil babies. My gerbil book says that it takes twenty-five days to make gerbil babies. I think they are already mating, because they act very affectionate to each other, so I will count today as DAY ONE and then I will observe them for twenty-five days and I hope that on DAY 25 their babies will be born.

This will be my Science Project.

Day Three.

My gerbils haven't changed much. They lie in their cage and sleep a lot. They're both overweight, because they eat too much, and they resemble Sonya Isaacson's mother, at least in chubbiness.

In personality, they resemble *my* mother. They're very grouchy.

Day Three Continued.

People who have serious emotional problems sometimes have difficulty doing real good gerbil-observation because they suffer from inability to concentrate. I myself have serious emotional difficulties so I have this problem.

As part of my Science Project I will talk about serious emotional problems. I will tell you what someone named Freud says about this.

The division of the psychical into what is conscious and what is unconscious is the fundamental premise of psycho-analysis; and it alone makes it possible for psycho-analysis to understand the pathological processes in mental life, which are as common as they are important, and to find a place for them in the framework of science.

Day Five.

My gerbils gave birth to premature babies. Instead of twenty-five days, it took them only five days to have babies.

Now I have eleven gerbils, and their names are Romeo, Juliet, Happy, Sleepy, Sneezy, Dopey, Grumpy, Bashful, Doc, Snow White, and Prince.

I also have a psychiatrist. His name is Freud. He is dead. But there is no need to be grossed out by that because with some psychiatrists it doesn't seem to matter much if they are alive or dead.

Day Twenty-five.

I have not written anything for a long time because I have felt very tired and it may be that I have a wasting disease. My dependent relations have no sympathy for someone with a wasting disease, I am sorry to say.

Here is what my psychiatrist says about dependent relations:

. . . the derivation of the super-ego from the first object-cathexes of the id, from the Oedipus complex, signifies even more for it. This derivation, as we have already shown, brings it into relation with the phylogenetic acquisitions of the id and makes it a reincarnation of former ego-structures which have left their precipitates behind in the id.

To identify my gerbils scientifically, I have colored their heads.

RED — ROMEO
BLUE — JULIET
YELLOW — HAPPY
GREEN — SNEEZY
ORANGE — BASHFUL
PURPLE — DOC

BROWN — GRUMPY
BLACK — SLEEPY
PINK — DOPEY
TURQUOISE — SNOW WHITE
WHITE — PRINCE

This will make it easier for me to know who is who, in case one of them has babies or something.

To identify my psychiatrist, I have put a large MAGENTA spot on his head. (There is, of course, no chance that my psychiatrist will have babies.)

Day Twenty-nine.

My gerbils have disappeared.

My gerbil book says this about disappeared gerbils: "If, in the process of escaping, the gerbils have been frightened, it is best to just sit very still in the middle of the floor until the gerbils come out of hiding on their own."

But my scientific assistant, Sam, and I sat very still in the middle of the floor for one hour, and my scientific assistant fell sound asleep while we waited. But the gerbils never appeared.

I think that by now there are eleven gerbils loose all over the house. And if my mother sees even ONE of them she is likely to have a nervous breakdown.

My mother doesn't even know I HAVE eleven gerbils.

And my psychiatrist is no help at all. He has his *own* problems: a villain has painted his nose blue.

Day Fifty-nine.

I have not worked on my Science Project for a long time because I have been extremely emotionally disturbed. One of the scientific things about gerbils is that they can cause you severe emotional problems.

My gerbils are all found and are back in their cage. Here is where they were found:

ROMEO (RED) — STUDIO, EATING A 4-H PENCIL
DOC (PURPLE) — STUDIO, EATING A 4-H PENCIL
JULIET (BLUE) — KITCHEN, EATING A RICE KRISPIE
HAPPY (YELLOW) — PILE OF LAUNDRY, EATING A TEE SHIRT
SNEEZY (GREEN) — VACUUM CLEANER INSIDES
BASHFUL (ORANGE) — COAL CAR OF OATMEAL-BOX TRAIN
GRUMPY (BROWN) — LEFT SLIPPER
SLEEPY (BLACK) — RIGHT SLIPPER
DOPEY (PINK) — STUDY, BEING A POLTERGEIST
SNOW WHITE (TURQUOISE) — SNEAKER
PRINCE (WHITE) — FLOWERPOT, EATING BEGONIA

Finding the gerbils has been a very traumatic experience for me.

My next scientific project will be finding a way to get rid of the gerbils. I plan to work very hard on this.

"Sigmund," said Anastasia, after she had checked the latch on the gerbil cage for the fifteenth time, "you haven't been very helpful to me through all of this."

She looked over at him. He didn't seem to be smiling anymore. He was staring at her with a stern look.

"What's wrong, Sigmund?" she asked.

Anastasia got up and went over to the head of Freud. The smile lines at the corners of his lips had begun to fade. He was getting his old mouth back, the one that looked serious and dour.

She reached for the black marker to replace his smile. Then she hesitated.

"Maybe it isn't a good idea to have a psychiatrist who always agrees with everything I say, and smiles," she told the head of Freud. "What do you think?"

He looked very sternly at her.

"Well, all right, you don't have to get *mad*," Anastasia grumbled. She went to her bed and lay down, staring at the ceiling.

"What would you do, Sigmund, if you had to get rid of eleven smelly gerbils?"

She glanced over. He was frowning.

"I know what you'd do," she said. "You'd probably

give them to someone you hated. You look as if you hate a lot of people.

"But I don't hate anyone that much," Anastasia sighed. "I used to hate my mother and father. That was a couple of months ago. But now I don't hate them anymore.

"Now I like them. My father was really nice when I told him about the gerbil problem. I suppose having all this psychiatric counseling helped me adjust to my parents."

Anastasia yawned. "And, of course, there were the hormones. But my hormones are gone, all of a sudden.

"First, the gerbils disappeared," she told Freud, yawning again, "and then the hormones did. Life is just one weird surprise after another."

eight

Anastasia trudged home from school with Meredith, Sonya, and Daphne.

"What do you guys want to do this weekend?" she asked her friends. "Go to the movies?"

"I want to hang out at McDonald's," said Daphne. "This guy in the ninth grade—Eddie Wolf—works there weekends. He's gorgeous."

"DAPHNE," said Anastasia grouchily, "you're becoming very boring. All you're interested in is guys."

"I told you," Sonya said. "It's Stage Two of adolescence. It's normal."

"Well, it's *boring,*" said Anastasia.

Meredith made a snowball and threw it at a tree.

"Guess what," she said. "I don't think it's boring. I think I'm entering Stage Two myself. I'll go to McDonald's with you, Daph."

"Not me," said Sonya. "I have to work on my science project. It's due in three weeks."

Anastasia kicked a chunk of snow. "Mine's just about done, but it isn't any good. I'm probably going to flunk."

"You can't flunk," Daphne pointed out. "Projects for the Science Fair are extra credit. You don't even have to do one. *I'm* not doing one. I don't have time."

"Yeah, because you're always out chasing guys," said Anastasia. "Here's my street," she added. "I'll see you. Call me if you want to go to the movies." She waved, and turned the corner toward her house.

"Hi, Anastasia!" Sam greeted her as she came through the back door. "Guess what? Nicky Coletti didn't come to nursery school today, so I had all the blocks to myself!"

Anastasia hung her jacket in the back hall. She sat down to unlace her snowy boots. "That's nice, Sam. Hi, Mom. Did you have a good day today?"

Her mother was at the kitchen counter, peeling

potatoes. Her back was turned. "No," she said, without looking around. "I did not."

Oh, great, thought Anastasia. Her mother was in a bad mood. Best to ignore her for a while; maybe it would go away.

"Whoops!" said Sam. "I almost forgot. Mom, my nursery school teacher sent you a note. It's here, in my pocket." He reached into his jeans and took out a piece of paper.

Mrs. Krupnik turned. Her face was very mad. "My hands are wet," she said. "Read it to me, Anastasia."

Anastasia unfolded the paper and read it aloud.

"Dear Early Learning Center Parents," she read. "One of our children, Nicky Coletti, has had an unfortunate accident and will be out of school for six weeks, with both legs broken. I'm sure the Coletti family would appreciate cards or small gifts, to make Nicky's convalescence easier."

Anastasia looked up. "Then it tells the Colettis' address," she added.

Sam had a broad grin. "Six weeks?" he said gleefully. "I don't get bashed over the head for six weeks?"

"Sure sounds that way," said Anastasia. "I wonder how she broke her legs."

"Probably kicking somebody," suggested Sam.

"Maybe climbing up someplace to smash a cookie jar," said Mrs. Krupnik, who was still upset about their blue cookie jar, which she had loved.

"I bet her father is a Mafia person," said Anastasia. "And he finally got mad and broke both her legs."

"We're being terrible," said Mrs. Krupnik, wiping her damp hands on a paper towel. "It's a shame, to have a child injured. I suppose we ought to send a card."

"A present," said Sam. "I'm going to send big fat ugly Nicky Coletti a present. I'm going to send her dog poop!"

"*Sam,*" said his mother sternly. "That's not nice."

Sam pouted. "I am," he muttered under his breath. "I'm going to send her a whole lot of smelly dog poop."

Mrs. Krupnik had gotten her angry face back. "Listen, you two," she said. "I've been waiting for you to come home, Anastasia, because I have something to discuss with you."

She reached up to a shelf beside the sink and took down a folded piece of paper. "I found this in the study this afternoon. And I want an explanation. I don't want any made-up excuses or stories or evasions. I want a full disclosure on this subject. And I want it RIGHT NOW."

Anastasia sighed, and sat down. She didn't have any idea what her mother was talking about. She didn't have any idea what the folded paper was.

But Sam, apparently, did. He was looking at it, and his eyes were wide. "Uh-oh," Sam said.

Mrs. Krupnik handed Anastasia the paper. It had typing on it—obviously Sam's typing, uncapitalized and all over the page.

Apprehensively, Anastasia read it:

```
                         gerbils!

gerbils*gerbils*gerbils*gerbils* gerbils* gerbils* gerbils*

1 2 3 4 5 6 7 8 9 10 11 gerbils

run gerbils run

            see gerbils go   see them run

my gerbils  my 11 gerbils  sam krupnik  run  run  run

help!!!!!  find the gerbils!!!  see them go hide!!!!
```

11 gerbils run up and down in and out help help help

find the gerbils ###&&&&@@@@*******

11 11 11 little gerbils! all

over

the

house!

gerbils!!!!!!!

"You really are getting pretty good at reading and writing, Sam," said Anastasia feebly. "And typing," she added.

"Does this mean what I think it means?" asked Mrs. Krupnik very grimly.

Sam was sucking his thumb vigorously.

"Well," Anastasia started, "in a way I guess it does."

"What do you mean, 'in a way'? Are there, or are there not, eleven gerbils?"

"Ah, yeah," said Anastasia, "there are."

"AND ARE THERE ELEVEN GERBILS RUNNING AROUND IN THIS HOUSE?"

"No," said Anastasia. "Definitely not. Not anymore, at least. We caught them."

"But they were. They *were* loose in this house, and you didn't tell me."

"That is correct," said Anastasia.

"I want them out of this house. Immediately. No arguments. No deals."

"Mom, I've been trying to figure out a way to get rid of them, something the Humane Society wouldn't arrest me for."

Sam took his thumb out of his mouth. He looked up. "I know a way," he said.

"Name it," said his mother.

Sam smiled happily. "We can send Nicky Coletti a lovely present," he said.

"This is terrible," said Mrs. Krupnik. "This is an absolutely malevolent, malicious, terrible thing to do. Hand me the Scotch tape, Anastasia."

She sealed the last corner of the wrapping paper over the gerbil cage.

"Here's the card," Anastasia said. They taped the get-well card to the top of the wrapped cage.

"All set, Dad," she said.

Dr. Krupnik lifted the cage and started out the door to the car. "I wouldn't do a rotten thing like this," he announced, "if that kid hadn't torn a page out of my first edition of Hemingway."

"Goodbye, gerbils," called Sam through the door as his father drove away.

"I hope they're happy in their new home," said Mrs. Krupnik. "Their raised ranch, with your wall-to-wall."

"Mrs. Coletti can deodorize it with your Avon florals," said Anastasia. "Because I have to admit, you were right, Mom: gerbils *do* smell."

"I feel terribly guilty," said Mrs. Krupnik. "I really am afflicted with guilt."

"If you want," suggested Anastasia, "I can provide you with a psychiatrist to help you deal with that."

"Freud?" asked her mother.

"He doesn't mind if you call him Sigmund."

"I thought you were still using him."

"I was, till just now. But my problems all seem to be gone. The gerbils are gone, and they were a big problem. And I don't hate you and Dad anymore. I think my hormones are gone."

"But what about your science project?" asked her mother.

Anastasia sighed. "It was for extra credit, anyway. I've decided not to do one."

"Sweetie, you could use the extra credit in science. You got a C in science on your last report card," her mother pointed out.

Anastasia thought about it. She didn't mind her C in science, really. But she knew her parents did. Suddenly, now that her parents had stopped being weird, she wanted to please them. And there did seem to be a solution, though she didn't like it much.

"Mom," she said with a sigh, "I have three weeks. If you helped me, I could probably do a big poster showing the life cycle of the frog."

"Sure. I could help you do that."

"But do you think the kids in my class would laugh? And if they *did* laugh, do you think I'd be mature enough not to mind?"

Her mother smiled and shrugged and shook her head. "Anastasia," she said, "why don't you ask your analyst?"